The Document Matters

Praise for
Nobody's Coming Home

"*Nobody's Coming Home* is a valentine to the Raymonds: Chandler and Carver. Minimalist, unsentimental, unflinching, character rich, this book is a must for anyone who loves crime stories, or just good writing."

-Chelsea Cain
New York Times Bestselling Author

"In *Nobody's Coming Home*, noir scribe Alec Cizak has his finger on the pulse of a society enduring rapid change—change for the worst. Stories like 'Destroyers' and 'The Old Pissing Wall' attack our collective apathy or ill-placed anger in a satire uniquely Cizak's. He is not only a first-rate writer, but also an authentic voice in a world coming unhinged. Cizak's prose is sharper than a blade held against your neck—he will give you the dreadful truth, and you will keep coming back for more."

- Matt Phillips, author of
Countdown, Know Me from Smoke, and *A Good Rush of Blood*

"A sleazy, bleak, and desperate collection of stories, and I mean that in a good way; Alec Cizak has gripped noir by the throat and throttled it to life in this paean to doomed, downtrodden humanity hoping the light at the end of the tunnel isn't a freight train. If you're a dark fiction fan, *Nobody's Coming Home* is a must-read to die for."

-Craig Faustus Buck, author of
Go Down Hard

NOBODY'S COMING HOME

by

ALEC CIZAK

ABC Group Documentation **//**
878 Mallory Drive
Marietta, GA 30062

The characters and events depicted in the stories in this book are fictitious. Any similarity to real persons, living or dead, is coincidental and not intended by the author.

Cover design by Eric Adrian Lee

Interior design by Jack Webster

ISBN: 1-957034-17-1
ISBN-13: 978-1-957034-17-1

This book is dedicated to DJ, Woody, Stuart, Shannon, Steve and everyone else I've considered a good friend who allowed themselves to be permanently seduced by the siren song of self-destruction. Your shadows haunt these stories the way you haunt my memories of younger, wilder days.

CONTENTS

PROGRESS

Late in the second hour of Jerry Springer, the stench bullied its way to her attention. She muted the TV and knocked on the door to the basement. Her son said, "What?" She opened the door and shouted down the steps.

"Time for your friend to leave, Junior."

"I'm not through with her." The snot in his voice begged for five across his mouth, as he'd often earned in his youth when he still had a father.

She could hear the clicks and clacks of the joystick in his hand, the rapid-fire gunshots of his video game. She descended the cackling, brittle steps. The girl's bluish legs poked from a clump of Sesame Street blankets at the foot of Junior's bed. How could the boy live with the smell? He'd wooed his previous girl until pieces of her threatened to fall off. Stuffing the sloppy corpse into a Spider-Man sheet and lugging it up the stairs had been hell. She'd sworn, then, she would not perform these minor tasks for the boy anymore. "You put that game on hold and listen to me."

Alec Cizak

The POV character on his flat-screen TV continued riddling Allied soldiers with bullets. He said, "Jawohl!"

"Junior!" She hated having to yell. Perhaps the girl's odor added to her irritation. "I want her out of this house, now!"

He paused the video game, stood, and kicked aside the blankets covering the girl's naked body. The girl had been a brunette, Junior's favorite. Her eyes stared through a jungle of dark, frizzy hair. He knelt and squeezed her thigh. "She's still got give, Mama."

"Stank she's letting off?" she said. "She's good and ready for the soil."

The boy wrapped his arms around his chest. He sat cross-legged and bit his lower lip, let her know she'd hurt his feelings. This had always been the point at which she caved, the point at which she found spare linen, rolled the corpse like a blintz pancake, hoisted it over her shoulder, and huffed it to the kitchen. After sundown, she'd head to the back yard. Whether she asked nice or barked, the boy would not help her dig the hole.

She sighed. She'd spoiled her son. She'd seen similar tragedies on Dr. Phil—grown children refusing to leave the house, refusing to get a job and pay their own bills. The celebrity shrink said Junior's generation suffered from a multitude of mental issues. And she'd gone along with it, believed the boy's insolence a product of having been born at an unfortunate point in history. "Where does it end?" she said.

"What you carrying on about?" The boy had used chocolate milk for his Cheerios again. Had a fudge-colored goatee, like he'd been five years old his entire life. He stroked the girl's pubic hair, pinched one of her butterscotch nipples. "I still like her, Mama."

Why couldn't she say no to him? Why couldn't she do what would have been best for both of them? She dropped her head in her hands and wept. "Junior, I just don't know anymore..." She turned and climbed the steps without looking at him. Maybe

2

getting rid of his father while the boy was growing up, maybe that'd been the problem. She didn't want to blame a dead man, however, for her current tribulations. She pulled a Bud Light from the fridge and ambled to the living room. Maury had started. More American trash reminding the audience life could get worse. She'd let it take her mind off her failure as a mother.

The beer floated her into a late afternoon nap. She'd have slept through Wheel of Fortune were it not for the foreign sound of her son struggling with something. The door to the basement opened and out walked Junior, his latest girlfriend twisted nice and snug in a Big Bird comforter, resting equal ways across his shoulders. He set the body down in the kitchen. As he returned to his room, he said, "Don't you worry, Mama. I'll plant her later, when it gets dark. Like you taught me."

She waited until he disappeared before leaking a different kind of tear. She wiped it away with her sleeve. She gloated to the losers on TV: Her son could be trained. Her son could grow. She granted herself visions of the boy acting like a man, fending for himself. Someday. Someday soon.

(2019)

MISCARRIAGE

Bob Cork had been adjusting information on a report about a gas station robbery. Captain ordered him to hustle over to the Korean War memorial. Bob finished typing corrected times on Liquid Paper and drove to the church across the street from the bronze statue of a charging soldier. A small crowd followed two people matriculating down Lincoln. He left his car behind a marked Lake County vehicle. A uniformed deputy kept the gawkers at bay. Bob joined the deputy to observe the main act:

A slim blonde, all legs, pockmarked skin, wearing denim shorts and a tie-dyed WLS T-shirt had duct-taped her hand to the grip of a silver revolver. The barrel of the gun rested inside the mouth of a taller man in a burgundy suit and tie. Duct tape held the barrel in place as well. The woman inched the man backward. Bob recognized her, though he couldn't recall from where.

He had no trouble identifying the man. Dan Rutter. Attorney at Baker and Barrett, a firm on 9th Avenue sliding rich folks through cracks in the code. When Bob worked sex crimes, he endured a trial designed to lock up a serial pedophile. The DA worked seven months to build the case. Dan Rutter and his cohorts grifted the jury with a boohoo about abuse the toucher suffered as a child. Didn't make sense to Bob how everyone else in the world managed their demons without hurting others. A reporter at Channel Five called him and the prosecutor heartless for casting a victim as a monster.

Brad Porter, the deputy, kept the minor crowd from the woman and the lawyer. Not even thirty, Porter's skin had grayed and his hair had thinned to strands jutting in lonely clumps from under his hat. Bob knew his father, police veteran and sharpshooter Butch Porter. Unlike his father, Brad Porter never put in for detective. Must have been content answering domestic calls and writing tickets. Like he knew advancing in the department would make the rest of his hair fall out. He beckoned Bob closer. "She abducted him at his office," he said. That's all anyone had at that point. Bob thanked him, told him to say hello to his father. "Pa'll be glad to know you're still kicking."

Bob fished a pack of Wrigley's spearmint gum from his pants pocket, unwrapped a piece and shoved it in his mouth. A poor substitute for the unfiltered Camels he'd forced himself to eighty-six a month earlier. He approached the lawyer and the woman. He held his hands where the woman could see they were empty. He let his shoulders slump, his belly sag over his waist. If he looked like a chump, maybe the woman wouldn't find him threatening. She sneered at him. "You don't want this turd's brains on that nice tweed jacket of yours, I suggest you skedaddle."

"Afraid I can't do that." With caution, Bob removed his badge from his inside breast pocket. "I'm a detective, ma'am. Just want to know what's going on."

The lawyer tried to speak. Muffled. Gibberish. "Hush," the woman said to him. To Bob, she said, "I'm taking this slime for a stroll. Folks need to know what he done to me and my daughter."

The lawyer shook his head. The woman kicked him in his shin. "My finger slips, you sleazy son of a bitch, your skull's an instant jigsaw puzzle." She laughed, said he'd have a closed-casket funeral. "No different from my little girl's." More muted protests from the lawyer. Must have been tough for him, unable to spit ten-cent bullshit, worm his way out of the situation. The woman turned to Bob. "This jagoff's going to apologize, publicly, on television." Bob asked how so. "It's happening already." Her hand taped to the gun twitched, prompting an unearthly squeal from the lawyer, a sound Bob heard in a science fiction movie about giant rats. "You jagoff cops are going to get Channel Five to bring one of their fancy cameras and we're going to listen to this prick sing." She nodded at the lawyer, as though Bob might not fathom which prick she meant.

"I'm happy to discuss this with you," said Bob. "But you insult folks, it's going to be difficult."

"Get on your little walkie-talkie, officer. Until I see a camera and microphone in this shitbag's face, this parade keeps on."

A regional barb cast Haggard, Indiana as a suburb of Chicago. A stupid joke, for sure, considering forty miles separated them. Sometimes, however, Bob wished he had Windy City resources. A tactical team would have been nice. Position units on the roof of the Art movie theater and have a deadeye incapacitate the woman. He didn't want to bring in the media, appease her. Every lunatic in town would take hostages to snag their fifteen minutes. "Ma'am," he said, "why don't you tell me your name?"

"Got nothing to say till I see that fancy news van."

"I need more information," he said. "Make it a lot easier for me to convince my captain to put in the call, get a camera here, like you want."

She stopped. "You don't know who I am?" She didn't wait for his response. "How long you been a pig?" How flattering. As though Bob Cork sold used cars for two decades and decided to become a cop after a midlife inquisition. "You never heard of Lita Lynn May?"

Bob almost extended a hand. "Lita? Good to meet you." He smiled. "I'm Bob C…"

"Lita's my daughter, shit-for-brains." She swallowed. "*Was* my daughter." She yanked the lawyer's head. "This tub of bile twisted shit every which way in court, got the demon who killed her off the hook without even probation."

Ah, yes. Now he remembered. One of several parents anxious to see Chad Bullock thrown over the wall. Son of Senator Ward Bullock, Chad spent time at IU Northwest before determining himself too smart for school. One of the few kids under the age of thirty who, in this year of our Lord, 1978, kept his hair short, his collars clean. He'd been accused of abusing women every which way. As in, the boy had issues with his mother and wouldn't rest until the women of Indiana understood his Oedipal rage. Could it even be called Oedipal? Didn't Oedipus love his mother? Chad Bullock beat a girl from Crown Point with an iron wedge. A piece of plastic would hold the girl's skull together for the rest of her life. He'd burnt the skin off two hookers from Lublin. And he'd stabbed Lita Lynn May in the face with a pair of sewing scissors. Ninety-nine times, according to the examiner. Bob knew the detectives who'd interviewed him. Every moment they spent in the tank with the little shit confirmed his guilt. Then Dan Rutter weaved his spell. Convinced the jury Chad Bullock's childhood, growing up in a castle near South Bend, left him scarred. Jury wanted the spoiled brat locked away in the Crossroads mental health facility in Gary. Rutter and his crew spoke with the judge, got the boy a vacation in Switzerland where, apparently, hanging out in the Alps cured psychotic tendencies. Poor Heidi. Poor Swiss.

Bob wondered how many of their women would be mutilated before they put the animal in a cage, where he fucking belonged.

Or maybe they'd gone all gooey on villains, the way Americans had for the last ten years. The woman had every right to hold the lawyer accountable. She led Dan Rutter into the street. Looked like she intended on heading toward Haggard Elementary, a one-story, red-bricked building full of children. More gawkers gathered. Bob said to Brad Porter, "Let's get these sheep out of here."

"Might take more than me."

"You got my say-so," said Bob. "Tell roll call what you need."

As the scene travelled, tiny step by tiny, cautious step, additional uniforms arrived. They dispersed the audience and played goalie any time an idiot wandered too close to the action. The woman said, "The hell you getting rid of the witnesses for?"

"Can't let anything happen to civilians," said Bob.

"What does that make me?" The woman's body jerked toward him. The lawyer produced a guttural squelch.

"I don't want anyone to get hurt," said Bob. "Least of all you. I know you've had it tough…"

"You ever lost a child?"

Not like her, he hadn't. His wife Judith miscarried in the early part of the decade. She'd blamed it on Nixon, the excitement of Watergate. Said Tricky Dick made her blood boil so bad her uterus evicted the baby. Bob went to see a doctor on his own. Learned his sperm didn't swim with vigor, enthusiasm. Doctor blamed the cigarettes. Bob kept the news to himself. Let Judith think, for the last four years, the failure had been hers.

He said to the woman, "No ma'am."

"Don't pretend you know my pain for a single moment's second."

"Yes, ma'am." He held his hands up again, as though she'd pointed the revolver at him.

She nudged the lawyer. He scraped his shoes on the pavement behind him, maybe feeling for impediments, rocks, potholes, things that might make him stumble, tug on the woman's arm. The woman kept her gaze on the world beyond the lawyer's bean-shaped head. She said, "Get me my camera, pig. This don't end until this here shitbag apologizes on television. I got to keep repeating myself, I might get tired and trip, you dig?"

Again with the sweet talk. Calling him a pig, expecting a favor. One he didn't believe he could fulfill. Captain would probably take a chunk of his ass, he caved to the woman's demands. The woman interrupted his thinking, said, "I don't see you on your little walkie-talkie, officer."

He excused himself and returned to his cruiser. He called Dispatch over the radio. "Put me through to the captain."

Upon hearing the details, the captain said, "The longer this goes on, the more sympathy she stacks." Bob agreed, asked for advice. "Can we run a reverse on her?" said the captain.

"I'm a basketball fan," said Bob.

"Trick her." The captain spoke in a soft voice, as though he believed Bob dumb enough to chat with him in front of the woman. "Diversion, Cork. Bullshit her. We let Rutter take a bullet, no telling what those weasels at B&B will put us through. In court *and* the filthy press."

Worried about the department's image. Great. Bob said, "Can we get a van from Channel Five?" They'd need a familiar reporter to go along with the grift. Camera. Mic. Everything had to appear on the level, convince the woman they respected her grief. He told the captain to put an armed officer behind the lens. A marksman.

"Dammit, Cork," said the captain, his voice still low. Bob informed him the procession had traveled a block south. The woman could not hear them. "Last thing we need is some sad sack broad eating a county bullet."

"She's angling for Haggard Elementary," said Bob.

The captain tossed the hot potato to him. "You decide, Cork. Consequences will be on your desk, not mine."

The uniforms diverted a herd of young folks, maybe students from Valpo. Shaggy hair, bell bottoms. Reeked of marijuana. Three of them in May the Force Be with You T-shirts. Fucking clones. Bob straightened his tie. He got back on the radio and instructed Dispatch. "Yes," he said, "Captain's okay'd it." He caught up with the woman and the lawyer.

The woman didn't face him when she spoke. "What's the story, officer?"

"Channel Five's on the way."

Sweat dripped in and out of pockmarks on the woman's cheeks. Had her face reflected the shitty cards life dealt her before her daughter died? So many Indiana women looked the same, including Bob's wife. Following the miscarriage, she stayed up late, forcing herself to laugh with Johnny Carson and other Hollywood phonies. The tiny black-and-white television in their bedroom hummed long after the National Anthem played and the station dropped to static. On Fridays, nights they'd previously reserved for baby making, she insisted on watching Graveyard Joe host cheap, scratchy horror movies on Channel Nine. Bob resorted to wearing a blinder and wrapping his pillow around his ears. Not long into this routine, Judith's skin deteriorated. He couldn't shake the hunch that his refusal to confess blame for the miscarriage contributed to her rapid aging.

Tammy Lynn must have been psychic, must have wanted to prod his conscience. She said, "What's on your mind, Officer?"

He nodded down 9th Street. "Here comes your camera, ma'am."

She steered herself and Dan Rutter in a straight line for Haggard Elementary's playground. Children laughed and screamed, ran

11

around in that bizarre way children did, finding joy in mindless movement. Several played kickball in the corner by a break in the high fence surrounding the blacktop. A group of girls and a boy skipped rope near the entrance to the school. On the opposite side of the kickball diamond, half a dozen boys played with plastic toy soldiers in a sandbox, mostly throwing sand at each other and laughing when one of them took some in the eyes.

"Ma'am," said Bob, "can I ask you to veer to the right?"

She turned her head. Must have seen the school. "Sure thing." She continued backing toward the opening in the fence.

"I thought I asked you to veer to the right?"

"You asked. That don't mean I got to comply."

"Ma'am, the children."

She stopped. Her smile lightened her weathered cheeks. "Yes?" she said. "The children?" She glanced at the playground. She snapped Dan Rutter's terrified face forward. "Nobody gave a shit about *my* child."

The news van parked across the street. Bob told the woman he needed to make sure Channel Five had followed his directions. The driver opened the sliding door. Inside, Cathy Moon, slender raven-haired former Notre Dame cheerleader, sat near a control panel, compact mirror in her hand, grooming her eyelashes. She glared at Bob. "Well, well. If it isn't the Salem witch hunter." He refrained from explaining a pedophile and someone wrongly accused of witchcraft in Puritanical America could not be equated. The other passenger in the van stepped out in jeans, cowboy boots, and a button-down shirt held together at the neck by a bolo tie. Time and experience had carved ravines in Butch Porter's face, turned it into a roadmap. He grinned and offered Bob his hand.

"Been a while," he said. "Detective, I hear?"

"That's right, Butch." Bob shook his hand and helped him pick up a camera and battery pack. Combined, they must have weighed seventy pounds. "You got instructions, right?"

Butch showed his right palm, revealed he'd worn a ring concealing the tiniest single-shot .22 Bob had ever seen. "Got this here rascal in Ko-rea."

Bob scratched his scalp. "You only going to need one bullet?"

"Impression I got from roll call," said Butch, "one is all it'll take."

The woman and the lawyer stood a few feet from the entrance to the playground. Teachers hustled students back inside the building. "She steps on school property," said Bob, "I'm going to need you to fire that shot."

Butch leaned around the front of the van. He gnawed on his lower lip as he stared at the target. "Tricky. Captain insisted nothing happens to the shyster."

Bob spit out his gum. His fingers ached to cradle an unfiltered Camel. He removed a fresh stick of Wrigley's and popped it into his mouth. As he chewed, he raised his eyebrows and shrugged. "Something happens to the woman," he said, "I don't see how the lawyer's not going to be affected."

After telling Butch and Cathy Moon to hold on a second, Bob weaved through meandering traffic, cars filled with rubbernecks, cars the uniforms should have redirected.

Scars on the woman's face appeared to have dug deeper, gathered more sweat. "That the bimbo from Channel Five?"

"She's won several awards, far as I know," said Bob. "I'm not mistaken, she's headed to Chicago in a few months. Earned a spot on the Channel Nine news."

"She's a dingbat," said the woman. "They put her on TV to get men to pay attention. She wears short skirts on assignment, always has perfect straight black hair. Like a smalltown Morticia Addams, but without the kinky wit."

"She's what we got." Bob tried to arc around her, stand between her and the playground.

The woman jerked the lawyer to the left, obstructing Bob's path.

"Now, ma'am…" He held his hands up for a third time. Felt silly doing so.

"Hey, pig," said the woman. "You told me you ain't lost a child like I did. I figure you're implying something."

"Don't you want to talk to the camera?"

"I see." She smirked. "You got yourself a dirty little secret, don't you? You chew gum to keep from spilling the beans?"

"Ma'am," said Bob, "all I ask is you stay off school grounds."

"I'll go where I damn well please."

Cathy Moon's narrow heels smacked the pavement until she stood next to Bob. He gave her room and loitered to the side of the sharpshooter. A cord attached to the battery pack slung over Butch Porter's shoulder snaked along the ground, up into the bottom of a microphone in Cathy Moon's hand. She looked at the camera and nodded. The reporter spoke into the microphone: "I'm standing outside Haggard Elementary where grieving mother…"

"You think I'm stupid?" Tammy pointed at the camera. "The little red light there, it ain't even on." She shoved the lawyer through the break in the fence and followed him onto the blacktop.

The pop from the gun wrapped around Butch Porter's ring finger sounded before the camera hit the ground. Bob closed his eyes, chomped twice on his latest stick of gum. He heard the second shot, competing with the echo of the first—two minor thunderclaps dancing on the walls of the school. When he opened his eyes, he stopped chewing. The sharpshooter had scraped a bullet across the woman's throat. She must have squeezed her revolver's trigger. The right side of the lawyer's face decorated the fence. The rest of him lay atop the woman. They convulsed in mingling puddles of blood.

"Jesus, Bob, I apologize," said Butch Porter. "I went for her wrist. Guess I ain't got it like I used to." His son, the deputy, rushed over, placed his hand on his father's back to comfort him.

Children on the playground shrieked and sobbed. Bob stared at the woman's fluttering eyes. She'd made a mistake. He knew *exactly* how she felt about losing her daughter. He returned to his car. He spoke into his radio, called for the necessary vehicles and personnel to clean the mess. He ducked away from the scene, walked toward a liquor store down the street. As he stepped into a phone booth at the edge of the liquor store's parking lot, he spit out his gum and dug through his pockets for a dime. The phone at his house rang three times before his wife answered. He said to her, "Listen, honey, we need to have a talk."

(2020)

POLITE SOCIETY

Gilbert got the call around seven. Normally, he'd ignore an anonymous number. Might be a johnny. But he'd just cashed a twenty rock and needed something to distract him from the crave. "Yo," he'd said.

"Gilbert?"

"Dave?"

"How's things?"

They shot the shit—Dave, talking about his oldest kid playing football; his daughter, the youngest, just started kindergarten. The middle one, *well you know how the middle child is,* quiet, not great, not terrible. Gilbert reminded him he had no kids, had no idea what he meant. He told him about his crappy life, being forty-seven and still living with his mother. "She gives me the business every time I bring a girl home."

"You still banging whores?"

"They're the only girls who'll give me the time."

"That's probably why she complains."

Dave said he needed help with something. Said Seth Short suggested he call him. Seth Short never picked Gilbert for gigs. Not since the last century. Not after Gilbert set up Seth's daughter with a bartender from Merrillville named Linden Sewell. Linden beat and raped her. Went missing the next day. Word Gilbert heard? Some of Seth's people, maybe Dave as well, scooped the scumbag off the street, took him to a warehouse, laid him out naked on one of those fancy dining room tables that split in the middle for an extension. They put Linden face down, his pecker dangling in the open space, brought in a hooker to suck him hard. Then two guys, maybe Dave and someone else, slammed the table together from both ends. Word Gilbert heard? Linden limped to the Greyhound station in Gary, got on the next bus to Atlanta, and never came back.

He said, "Sure, Dave," feeling honored. Feeling like, maybe, just maybe, Seth Short might give him more work. He used to let him drive his Caddie to and from Chicago, loading and unloading smack. Used to let Gilbert hang out in his condo in Valpo. They'd shoot heroin, cocaine, anything they could pull into a needle. Listened to Janis Joplin records and talked about a revolution that never happened. Things seemed better. Glamorous, maybe. He still lived with his mother then, sure, but she didn't get in his face all the time, telling him to do something with his life.

Dave rolled up in a sparkling Caddie. Gilbert stood outside, waiting. He got in the car. It smelled like pine trees. Dave looked clean as ever. No stubble on his chin, no wrinkles at his eyes or on his forehead. Gilbert stared at his own belly, a glob of blubber resting between his chest and his lap like a giant globe. *Disgusting.* He'd dressed in cargo shorts and a T-shirt with holes under both armpits, a shirt his mother tried to eighty-six any time he let her do his laundry. And here sat Dave, decked out in jeans, a clean Oxford, and a leather jacket.

"Good to see you," he said to Dave.

"Good to see you, Gilbert."

He said his name so formal. It bothered him. In the old days, they'd had a million nicknames for everyone in the gang. They called Gilbert Stinky because he carried a spare tire big enough for a monster truck and smelled like bong water. They called Dave Slick. A player, always corking the latest tail to stroll Temple Boulevard. He even nailed Bible Lisa, a holy roller/punk rocker who teased every prick in Lublin and Haggard to the point of contact before pulling her up panties and insisting she wasn't *that* kind of girl. Dave did her at a guy named Kyle's house and Kyle'd told everyone. Enough rumors followed to send Bible Lisa on her way to Kentucky, where she no doubt tried once more to convince the world she remained a virgin.

Dave put the car in drive. He fiddled with the radio. "What you listening to?"

Gilbert said, "WLS's cool."

"Shit," said Dave. "They've been playing the same four Zeppelin songs since the fucking seventies." He turned the dial to a Valpo station. Classical music.

"This crap's for old people," said Gilbert.

Dave increased the volume.

They cruised west. Streetlamps cut a steady pattern of light and dark across the windshield. Dave complained about a PTA meeting his wife insisted he go to earlier. "You wouldn't believe the things these teachers ask for," he said. "I mean, shit, they don't need books for each student when the damn kids can just snap a picture of the pages they're studying on their goddamn phones. I wish these fucking teachers would get with the times."

Gilbert said, "So what's the deal? What's the gig, already?"

19

"Nice," said Dave. "Straight to business. I dig that. I've always dug that about you." He opened the glove box. "There's a straight-shooter and a couple of rocks, you want to get your mind comfy."

"You smoking?" said Gilbert.

"Give me a break," said Dave. "I got a family, bills, shit..."

Gilbert took his time loading a lung buster. He hit the pipe and closed his eyes. Top notch. A clean cook. It didn't rocket him to Mars, like the first time he'd tried crack, back in the nineties. Nothing ever did or would. The methane odor stirred his memory, made him *think* he'd gotten that high again. "Good stuff," he said when he exhaled.

"It's Seth's," said Dave. "Of course it's good."

Ah, polite society Dave. Gilbert, while not saying so, had some problems with him. The few times he'd seen Dave since that fall in ninety-nine, he'd had a snoot about him. Heck, he'd introduced Dave to Seth Short in the first place. He'd introduced him to Seth Short's daughter, Heather. And while he'd wanted more than anything to make love to Heather, to slobber all over her giant boobs, to bang her doggy style with her wavy brown hair wrapped around his fist, he hadn't said a word when Dave went ahead and corked her first. Heather didn't sleep with a guy and later spread for one of that guy's friends. Some bizarre moral code. That's what compelled Gilbert to set her up with the bartender. Someone who associated with people she'd never met.

"All right." Dave turned onto Ninth Avenue and headed north. "So, you know JoJo, dude in a wheelchair, tiny legs? Not a midget or anything. Shit, not sure what the fuck he is. Lives in one of those hippie buses, works birthday parties, making animals and shit with balloons?"

"Crackers the Clown," said Gilbert. "Sure, sure."

"That guy calls himself Crackers?" Dave shook his head like a hoity-toity talk show twat. "He spends all the money he earns off those children on his fucking drug habit, you know that, right?"

"Sure, sure," said Gilbert. Of course he knew that. JoJo'd never sold out. Long after the frat boys and sorority girls from Valpo ruined Lublin with their drunken nonsense, long after the Chicago brothers learned blitzed white girls looking to get plugged populated Lublin nights, long after the arts-and-crafts shops had closed and been replaced with one stupid yuppie beer hole after another, JoJo continued parking his van in the alleys behind the bars and living the life he'd always lived. Nothing but respect for him. One of the only people from the old days Gilbert could rely on for dope and company.

"Well, JoJo's been making a habit of pissing off Seth," said Dave. "First thing this dumb fuck does, he sells him an eight-ball that turns out to be a fucking cashew or something. A fucking nut, wrapped in cellophane to look like an eight-ball. Can you fucking believe it? I mean, if I were a fucking cripple, last thing I'd do is give Seth Short an excuse to be pissed off. I'm just saying, that's me."

"That's a stale trick," said Gilbert. "Wrapping a peanut in cellophane, that's ancient. You remember Paul, used to sell bunk acid to skater punks back in the nineties? He moves fake rocks all over the place."

"Funny you should mention Paul," said Dave. "He shows up in part two of this story. So, Seth unwraps this fucking peanut. Why the fuck Seth is fucking around with that shit, who the fuck knows? Man's got cancer. Who the fuck knows how long he's got to live. I guess he's squeezing what he can from what he's got left. Something like that, I hope. He figures out as soon as he fires it up, it ain't no fucking cocaine. So, I get the job of finding JoJo and bringing his crippled ass to Valpo."

"Seth couldn't get any dope down there?"

"Things weren't happening, what can I say? Valpo is all about pills since, shit, the fucking century flipped. Crack don't do it for those boys. Seth Short and, well, JoJo and Paul and, I guess, *you*, you're all relics. Don't ever tell Seth I said so, but somebody fucks around with crack, at this point, they deserve whatever fucking brain damage they end up with."

Gilbert said, "And pills are better?"

"The fuck you talking about?" Dave slapped him in his ear. "*All* that shit's for losers."

"Whatever." Gilbert loaded another rock into the straight-shooter and hit it. A spark hopped from the broken car antenna and landed on his ratty shirt. He snuffed it, but not before it left a fresh burn mark.

"Back to the story," said Dave. "I couldn't get a hold of you that night, so I had to do some detective work on my own. I find out Paul's gotten JoJo in on his best moneymaker, you know, selling his fucking mouth to queers on Hatcher Avenue. So, I go uptown, find the both of them hooking right by that toy store, like that isn't something fucking blasphemous or what, I mean, fucking parents bring their kids into that place, they fucking *shop* there. So, I point a Glock at them and tell them to get into the car. Take them to Seth's and Seth threatens to dump them into Lake Michigan if they don't give him back twice what he paid for the fucking peanut. They piss and moan, say it's all the money they've made sucking dick that night, can't they have some sort of payment plan? And this, this is what I don't get—they somehow work a deal to move shit for Seth down the road."

"Seth hired *them*?" Gilbert looked out the windshield. The lights of the High Note nightclub flashed in the distance. Young people mixed it up under the marquee. JoJo'd said nothing to him about working for Seth Short. Or giving head on Hatcher Avenue. Or that he'd hung out with Paul. Again.

"Sure," said Dave. "Seth tells them to move eight-balls for him. *Real* eights, that is. They sell them for two hundred, they keep fifty. That's the sweet deal Seth, for whatever fuck-all reason, that's the deal he gives these fuckos. Shit, maybe he wants to take over the north side. Hell, I just don't know. Well, those bozos couldn't even get it right once. Seth handed them a dozen eights and told them to have his money yesterday or they wouldn't be doing nothing no more ever again, know what I mean?"

"Yesterday's come and gone," said Gilbert.

"Sure has." Dave pulled into a small lot behind a former Masonic lodge. The Masons sold the four-story building years ago. Frat boys stuffed their faces with beer and wings at a BW3 on the ground floor. Their girlfriends bumped and grinded with brothers from Chicago in a dance club on the top levels. The brick walls thumped to monorhythmic noise. Dave said, "You in?"

"What?"

He opened his door. "Step out here for a minute."

Gilbert followed him to the back of the car.

"Ladies and gentlemen," said Dave, "Mr. Fabulous!" He opened the trunk. Paul Larson's dead eyes stared into the night. His face had been beaten purple and black. Dave reached past the body and produced an orange plumbing wrench. "I need you to help me find JoJo."

"I'm not that kind of guy." Gilbert looked at his hands for the crack pipe. He'd left it in the glove box, of course.

Dave shook his head. "That's why," he said, "that's why, my man." He shut the trunk.

Gilbert considered walking home. All the way from Lublin. A young man, maybe in his early twenties, ballcap turned backwards, Greek letters on his sweater, stumbled around the side of the Mason building.

"'Sup, brah," he said to Gilbert. Then he leaned into a row of bushes and ralphed.

Someday that kid would get a job. A suit-and-tie routine. He'd kiss the ass of an older version of himself. He'd make money, never have to live with his parents. Marry a girl who'd be gorgeous just long enough to squirt a few kids. And then they'd all rot over the decades, clinking wine glasses at symphony shows or talking Shakespeare and neo-liberal politics at hoity-toity plays. Everyone around them would look just the same and none of them would notice.

He got in the car. "I'll help you find him," he said. "That's it, though."

"That won't impress Seth," said Dave.

"I might still change my mind about the whole thing."

Dave nodded toward the glove box. "Take another hit, *Stink*."

They parked in the moon-induced shadows of a tree behind the old library. Gilbert said JoJo usually settled for the night across the street. "Remember how we used to duck back there," he said, "all of us, back in the day, passing a doober?"

"Long time ago." Dave rolled down his window, rested his elbow half in and half out of the car. "Between making money for Seth and taking my kids to school, I don't get a moment to myself, not even for a simple puff of weed."

"That's sad," said Gilbert.

"It's called being grown up," said Dave. "For Christ's sake, how are you going to get your shit together, you don't even know what it's like to make payments on a mortgage? You have any idea what it's like to take your son to his first Bears game? These are the things that give life *meaning*."

"I don't care about basketball."

24

"Jesus," said Dave. "You going to be living with your mother when you're sixty?"

Gilbert finished the rock in the glove box. His heart beat too fast. He had the shakes. But he didn't feel high, per se. Of course. Maybe another rock, maybe even just one more hit, right then, right there, maybe that would do the trick. He said to Dave, "You think I'm happy, where I'm at, you think I'm happy? You think that's what I want?"

"Seth Short'll take you back in a snap, Stink." He adjusted the air-conditioning.

"You remember sitting in your room, in your dad's house, back in '90, or maybe '91?" said Gilbert.

Dave said, "I don't remember much of anything between '85 and '96."

"We used to listen to Nirvana, before the frat boys ruined them," said Gilbert. "Remember? Remember *Bleach* and Black Flag and the Circle Jerks and Bad Brains, G.G., Bill Hicks, freaking *Goodfellas* and *Natural Born Killers*? Remember how we'd drink tequila every night, smoke weed, how we used to talk about how dead the yuppies were, how pointless it must be to punch a clock and turn your woman into a baby factory, how we made fun of those losers at Little League games, drunk in the stands, starting fights over whose brat was out or safe at home plate, how putting your hand over your heart and worshipping Old Glory was just a remake of *Triumph of the Will...*"

"Stink," said Dave, "we were eighteen. Stoned and stupid. You think I don't remember all that shit about knocking over Uncle Sam? It was bullshit. All we ever did was get wasted and scour the village for hungry puss. Kids today, kids in their twenties, they talk the same stupid shit. They think they're the first to discover the joy of sticking your dick in a wet pussy, they think they're the first to realize bigotry and that old-world shit is for the fucking birds, and they're no different than we were. Those with common sense will get married, make babies, and live the fucking life you're supposed to live. Unless you want to die a stupid death or, even dumber, get your stupid ass thrown in jail. You either go with the flow, Stink, or you fucking sink like the goddamn Titanic."

"I still think society can change." Gilbert flicked the lighter and burned coke residue in the straight-shooter.

"And that's why, brother, that's why…"

The hideous rumble of an engine untended for years filled the air. The smell of exhaust washed out the aroma of methane from the crack pipe. A rusted white-and-green VW bus, clothes hangers barely holding the side door in place, pulled into the lot by the library.

"There he is," said Dave.

"There he is," said Gilbert.

The side door to the bus rattled open. JoJo Walker pushed his wheelchair out. He climbed down and got into it. He fumbled with a pile of junk in the middle of the van, found a Coleman lamp and lit it. Shadows of bare branches flickered against the library's brick walls.

Dave said, "Go on over there, get him talking, get him comfy."

Gilbert stared at his hands. He could have pulverized Dave if he wanted. Maybe. He'd never seen him fight with his fists. He usually just clobbered people with a hammer or tire iron or, apparently, a plumbing wrench.

"The fuck you waiting for?" Dave slid the wrench up his jacket sleeve.

On the walk across the street, Gilbert considered telling JoJo to get back in the bus and drive as far away from Lake County as possible. Maybe JoJo had a weapon. Maybe even a gun. He'd tell him to shoot Dave as soon as he got out of the Caddie.

"Stinky!" said JoJo. He wheeled over, gave him some play. "You look good, brother."

"What's up, Crackers." Gilbert choked a bit. Maybe sadness, maybe anger. He wanted to warn him, but he said, instead, "Paul? You? *Hatcher Avenue?*"

JoJo dropped his head. "I needed the green, my man."

The door to the Caddie opened. Dave's polished boots spanked the sidewalk. "JoJo Walker," he said, "your life is calling."

Gilbert expected JoJo to wheel away. But his friend only stared up at him. No expression on his face. He said, "They get Paul?"

Dave pushed Gilbert out of the way. JoJo tried to scream. Dave cracked him in the mouth with his fist. The wrench dropped from his sleeve, clanked on the ground. He grabbed a handful of JoJo's shirt and dragged him off his wheelchair and over the concrete. He hit the trunk button on his keychain and threw JoJo on top of Paul. Then he slammed the lid.

Gilbert got in the car. He turned away from Dave. Scrunched his nose to avoid sniffling.

"Where's the wrench?" Dave put the key in the ignition and fired up the engine. "The fucking wrench, you left it on the street?" He got out and marched to the parking lot.

Just reach over, press the button for the trunk. But JoJo would barely be able to climb out before Dave returned. Gilbert rubbed his eyes. He turned toward the back of the car and said, "I'm sorry, man."

JoJo's little fists beat the walls of the trunk. Hardly made a sound.

Dave drove like a grandma to Valpo. Gilbert said, "Seth going to talk with JoJo?" The coke made his arms restless. He wiped his palms on his knees.

Dave said, "You kidding me?" He turned onto Temple. The stench of Lake County Animal Control's cremation plant invaded the car. Smelled like a thousand decaying corpses took a dump at the same time.

"Oh," said Gilbert. Seth had told him once how they had friends working for the county. When they needed to get rid of somebody, they shoved them into the furnace, right along with stray dogs and cats nobody wanted.

They pulled into a lot behind the plant, parked in a row of unmarked vans. White smoke roiled from the stacks overhead. Gilbert could barely breathe.

Dave said, "I'll take the cripple, you carry Paul." He opened the trunk and hoisted JoJo out the same way he'd scraped him across the street in Lublin. JoJo tried to bite his arm. Dave drew back and slammed him into the concrete. JoJo bounced and flopped like a rag in the wind. Dave said to Gilbert, "Get the fucking fruitcake."

Rigor mortis had set in. Pulling Paul's huddled corpse out of the trunk proved an exercise in geometry. Gilbert enjoyed bonking the guy's head on the car as he positioned his arched body over his shoulders. He followed Dave into the cremation plant. Then it came to him:

"I'll cover it," he said.

Dave stopped. "What?"

"JoJo's tab with Seth, I'll cover it."

"How the fuck you going to come up with that kind of money?"

"I'll ask my mom."

Dave shook his head, opened the door, and forced JoJo through it.

Gilbert turned sideways to get Paul's body into the building. An older man, maybe in his fifties, wearing a gray T-shirt with the name Red stitched onto the breast pocket, said hello. "Let's get this show on the road," he said. "Super's coming back real soon." He led them to a caged elevator. They squeezed onto it, Red pushing the LL button while helping keep JoJo under control. He glanced at Gilbert, smirked. He said to Dave, "How's Angie?"

"Same old, same old," said Dave.

"The kids?"

"Eh, you know."

"Tell me about it," said Red. "Got a call from my ex-wife. She tells me my oldest is shaking her tits at Sugar Cookies. The hell am I paying her tuition for if she's going to end up being a floozy like her mother?"

"Tell me about it," said Dave.

The elevator rocked to a stop. Red slid the doors open.

Gilbert pinched his nose. Men stood around stacks of dead cats and dogs, shoveling them into one of six giant, iron furnaces. It didn't seem possible so many stray animals actually existed in Lake County.

"Boys," Red said to a group of men working near the oven closest to the elevator. They got the hint and moved to the next pile of animals. Nobody seemed to notice Dave, clutching JoJo, who struggled, clawing at Dave's hands, or Gilbert, with a dead man draped around his shoulders. They must have seen any and everything chucked into the ovens.

Red used a hook to open the throbbing door on the furnace as wide as possible. "Let's get that big fellow in here." He grabbed Paul's legs. Gilbert took his arms. "On three." They swung the body and let go. Paul's corpse flew ten feet before landing with a thud and hissing as flames caught it.

"Here you go." Dave handed Gilbert the plumbing wrench. "I'll hold the midget still, you give him a good one on the noggin."

Gilbert stared at the wrench. He couldn't tell if the discolorations on it were rust or dried blood.

JoJo shrieked. He cried Paul's name, over and over. Gilbert raised the plumbing wrench, imagined JoJo was Paul. *That's who you're mad at.* He dropped the wrench on the floor.

"I can't do it."

"Christ." Red slapped himself in his forehead. "Who's Seth working with these days?"

Dave handed JoJo off to Red and picked up the wrench. "This is why," he said to Gilbert. "This is fucking why." Then he bashed JoJo three times in the face. Showered the floor with blood and tooth fragments. Some of it got on Gilbert's shirt, blended with coffee and ketchup stains on his chest.

Whether he'd died or not didn't matter. Dave and Red threw him into the fire, on top of Paul. Gilbert couldn't smell anything. He couldn't hear anything. His skin numbed. He ran his fingers up and down his arms. He couldn't *feel* anything.

As they drove back up Temple, Gilbert brooded the way he did any time his mother scolded him for bringing a hooker to the house. When the classical music on the radio got mellow, he said, "I'm sorry."

Dave slowed in front of Gilbert's mother's house. He didn't put the car in park, he just kept his foot on the brake. "Take it easy, Gilbert."

Gilbert tried to sneak inside. His mother lounged in the living room, knitting a blanket she'd been working on for several years. Lotion she smeared on her hands all the time made the house smell like strawberries. "What you been up to?" she said.

"You know," he said, "stuff, whatever."

She made a noise, like, *That's what I thought.* "You still wearing that nasty shirt?" She put her needles down. "Least I don't have to listen to you hammering away on a prostitute," she said. "At least that's something."

"That is something." He sat next to her and turned on the TV. Sarah McLachlan pleaded for donations to an animal charity. Broken cats and dogs moped for the camera.

"Lord," said his mother, "I don't want to see that."

"Who does?" said Gilbert. He changed the channel.

(2015)

CRANK BAXTER AIN'T NO GODDAMN CHRISTIAN

Some guys folded the moment Crank Baxter slipped Betsy, his brass knuckles, over his fingers. He considered them smarter than the average chump. The average chump, of course, couldn't have been too bright in the first place. Ending up in Seth Short's warehouse, limbs tied to a metal folding chair, meant you'd done something stupid. Meant you deserved a snapped femur or a dislocated kneecap or maybe a fractured skull. Seth had patience. He gave junkies opportunities to straighten the book. Spoke in a soft voice while chain-smoking Cohiba cigarillos. He understood the times, the economy. A chump landed in the warehouse on account of his own stubbornness. Or idiocy. Either way, it didn't bother Crank. Doing what he did. Slamming a chunk of steel against the side of a chump's face moved him in no way. Neither did the ensuing cries, the pleas. Tears, blood, spit, sloshing down a chump's jacket, crafting puddles on the concrete floor. Difficult to earn money these days, why worry about the means?

On a Thursday, a week out from Christmas, Seth called Crank to the warehouse to work on a chump named Mitch. Twig-shaped junkie who'd survived on scams, doing Seth favors in exchange for a fix. But the favors ran thin. Seth fronted Mitch to keep withdrawal from killing him and soon realized the chump couldn't settle the bill. He offered suggestions, said the chump should go to Chicago and hustle himself to perverts. Mitch refused. Seth explained he needn't follow through, rather, he could knock the johns unconscious and rob them. Mitch said he didn't have that in him. Seth asked if he'd be willing to drive a rental car full of guns to the south side of Chicago. Mitch peddled a conscience angle, said, "I don't want to add to the carnage." Like anybody had a choice in the way the puppet masters spun society, rich or poor. Seth gave him twenty-four hours to produce a down payment.

Mitch tried to run. Bugle Stork, another hired fist, helped Crank retrieve Mitch from the sewer in Haggard. High school kids and junkies enjoyed their poisons in the fetid caverns. Probably got off staring at emerald reflections of water drawing psychedelic patterns on the concrete ceiling. Bugle's bulbous nostrils heaved like lungs as he carried Mitch sideways out of the tunnel and jammed him into the back of Seth's cream-colored Buick. During the ride to the warehouse, Mitch promised everyone in the car he'd get the cash. Seth, behind the wheel, said, "I know you will, Mitch. I know you will." The vehicle continued toward the outskirts of Lublin, to a stretch of land covered with dead knee-high grass, dirt parking lots, and abandoned aluminum structures industry used when industry still existed. Mitch jammed his face in the window and wept.

He stumbled, on his own, with Crank, Bugle, and Seth, across the uneven parking lot and through the bent sky-blue door of the warehouse. Crank and Bugle secured the skinny man's arms and legs to the folding chair with duct tape. His chest rose and sank, rose and sank. An engine, revving, desperate to get things started. Seth stood by a cracked window, chomping a cigarillo. He gave

Mitch the speech, let him know things had moved beyond personal feelings, allegiances, good memories. It now made economic sense to pay guys to deliver an unpleasant impression. Business had to be attended to; "You remember Crank from high school, I'm sure." He sounded like a father explaining to his preteen son, just before beating him with a belt, why throwing lit firecrackers into church during service is unacceptable. "As your brain dances with pain, your creative instincts will take over. I want you to use that moment to think about ways you can get my money." He nodded to Crank. "Try to leave a few of his teeth where they belong."

On the way home, Crank stopped off at a Family Express. Outside, a man in a wheelchair held up a Folger's can. He wore the same filthy, tattered brown suit every day. Smelled like a port-a-potty at the Indy 500. "Help a brother?" Crank shook his head. How many times had he refused to give the man money? Why didn't the dirty codger figure it out?

He pushed through people inside the convenience store. Some made noise until they got a look at him, at which point they skedaddled like they'd spotted a tornado. He nabbed a bottle of B&R root beer from the cooler section to nurse his knuckles, bruised from Betsy digging into them. He also bought purple grape-flavored Boone's for his girlfriend, Yulia. If he could get her drunk before she started yapping about her day, he might grab a night of quiet, a night he could spend painting a plastic model '67 GTO he'd glued together over the weekend. He wanted to sit at his table by the window in their apartment, listen to his Sinatra playlist on YouTube, and go to bed at a decent hour. Yulia liked staying up late, watching movies on Netflix. Not the good ones, the old ones, rather, the recent crap. Thankfully, they were so awful, he had no trouble falling asleep while she sat next to him, giggling at jokes nobody who worked for a living would ever find humorous.

She greeted him at the door in yellow panties and a midriff-exposing Smurfette T-shirt. She gave him a smackeroo on the lips and took the Boone's from his hand. "Missed you, baby," she said. "You wouldn't believe what's trending on Twitter."

"Why don't you break that open, there." He nodded at the bottle.

Her face collapsed into a pout, the kind college girls wore for selfies posted on social media. "You in one of your moods?"

He pulled a wooden chair with one wonky leg from under the table by the window. "I just want to relax."

"You say that every night." She opened the lid on the Boone's and downed a third of it.

"Make that last," he said.

She sat on the edge of their bed, a fold-out couch never used as a couch. "It would be awesome," she said, "if you could drop the grumpy-old-man routine for, I don't know, a day? How about a week?"

"I'm not a grumpy…"

She rolled on her side. Laughed at him. When she composed herself, she said, "Crank, beyond the night we met and came back here to screw, I've never seen you smile."

"So…what are you doing with me anyway?"

The pout returned. "I know you're a good guy," she said. "You just put on this show because, I don't know. You do something nasty for a living, I know that much."

"Don't start…"

"I'm not going there." She raised her hands like someone being mugged. "I just wonder if you might not think about it. Think about looking at the world differently. Instead of walking around a big angry gorilla, be that gentle giant kids look up at with awe."

36

He chuckled before he could stop himself. "That'll be the day." Frank Sinatra crooned over the tiny speaker in his phone. Crank examined the model GTO the way a jeweler handled a diamond ring. This seemed to send a message to Yulia. She whisked her frizzy hair to the side and grunted. As Crank opened a tiny jar of metallic blue paint and dipped a brush in it, he considered his attraction to the woman. Her displeasure with his getting lost in his hobby represented the worst of her temper. As he turned the GTO metallic blue in careful, gentle strokes, he noticed her staring at him. He said, "What?"

"I just wonder," she said, "if a man capable of transforming these little plastic cars into works of art is really beyond hope."

Seth called at eleven the next morning. "Got a chump likes to smack his girlfriend around for the usual stupid shit. Girl won't press charges. Her brother wants us to have a conversation with the chump. We already got him. Meet us at the place in twenty."

On his way to Lublin, Crank stopped off at the Family Express for a root beer. The man in the brown suit had parked his wheelchair by the door again. Crank sighed as he got out of his car, a compact Chevy. Should have sent a signal to the bum: Crank did not have money. He barely made rent and other bills on the cash he picked up, tax-free, busting skulls. In his mind, Yulia's voice interrupted him: "You have a roof over your head, he does not." The guy couldn't even walk. Had to be a story. Crank dug in his pockets, found two quarters, a nickel, and three pennies. Change from the previous day's trip to the convenience store. As he approached the man, he hoisted the corners of his mouth into a smile. God, he hated people who smiled all the time. Especially men. His father never smiled. His grandfather never smiled. They'd died young. Grandpa at sixty-two. His father at forty. Both worked at Liberty Steel. Witnessing their rotten lives convinced Crank to earn his bread elsewhere. Satisfied he'd twisted his face into something resembling nice, he angled for the man in the wheelchair.

"Morning." Something odd lurked in his greeting. Pleasant tones. Yuck. He held out his hand with the change in it.

The man in the wheelchair looked at him, eyes slim, like he didn't trust him. "You kidding me?" Gravel laced his voice, a rough noise dredged from an existence, Crank assumed, of endless disappointment. A real man, Crank's father would have said. "How many times you passed me up like I'm a piece of shit, a near-invisible obstacle to buy your fucking root beer?" He grabbed the change from Crank's hand and counted it. "You serious?" he said. "Can't even get White Castle with this…" He turned away.

Crank's first thought: Pick up this ungrateful piece of shit by the collar of his filthy button-down shirt and throttle him. Introduce his smudged face to Betsy. Add some crimson to the gray coat of dust covering his skin. Yulia, no doubt, would forgive the man without deliberation. Can you blame him for being angry, bitter? Crank understood anger. This allowed his mind to loop around to the kind of logic Yulia entertained. He fished a money fold from his pocket. Mostly twenties held together with a silver clip fashioned to look like a striking cobra. He found a five-dollar bill. Surely that would cover breakfast at a fast-food joint. Hell, the Family Express sold wrapped Italian subs for three bucks. Even had a microwave to heat it.

The man snatched the money, his grime-covered hand moving with the swiftness of a snake. "That's more like it." He offered a crooked smile, demonstrated the same hesitance Crank had crafting his own. Something they had in common—a general distaste for civility. The man wheeled himself out of his way.

Crank navigated crowded aisles of Hostess products and other poisons to the coolers. As he grabbed the fifth root beer in line, he glanced outside the large windows along the far end of the store, by the front doors. The man in the wheelchair stood and folded his wheelchair together. He picked up the wheelchair with one hand and raced across the street, toward a 21st Amendment liquor store. Crank wanted to chase after him, catch him by the collar of his shirt and strangle him.

No, no, he heard Yulia say. If the man is an alcoholic, he's sick. She would know. The woman guzzled cheap wine day and night.

No, no, he told himself. We're smiling. We're painting our world in Disney colors. Brighter than any model car in his collection. We're learning to enjoy life. All the time. Instead of unleashing a torrent of profanity and beating the bum half to death, he forced himself to laugh. What a wonderful, ironic joke. If he'd believed in God, he'd chalk it up to a moral lesson. He ignored teenagers grabbing cans of Atomic Fuel two coolers down, gawking at him as he forced the choppy music of amusement from his vocal cords. The staccato chuckles of a lunatic.

The horrid croak of his laughter continued in the car. He drove through Haggard to Lublin, to the outskirts, and parked next to Seth's Buick in the dirt lot surrounding the warehouse. As he adjusted his plain, black T-shirt on the way to the door, he told himself, We need to get our shit together. He couldn't get past the scene with the bum, however. The mechanical, purposeful transition from helpless invalid to trickster. Just a snap of the fingers. Brilliant, in a certain way.

Yes, yes. Let's consider the grifter an artist.

This cleared his thoughts as he entered the warehouse. Seth stood near a broken window smoking a cigarillo. He exhaled through the jagged hole in the busted pane. He used the Cohiba to direct Crank's attention to a slim man tied to the bloodstained folding chair. "Others got hungry, went to Popeye's in Merrillville. At least, said they were." He puffed on the cigarillo and blew granite fog into a fractured beam of sunlight. "Got tired of waiting for you, I guess."

"Had an episode on the way over." Crank pulled Betsy from his pocket and slipped her across his knuckles.

"Tell me about it later."

The chump wore skinny jeans and a tawny knit sweater. Smelled as if he'd soiled himself. Crank assumed he worked in a bookstore or coffee house. Probably both. Probably an English major, pissed he'd dug himself a crater of debt from which he'd never recover. He'd grown a long, unkempt beard, as did all the clones claiming to be hip. He sobbed quietly, his halted grunts not too different from Crank's laughter in the convenience store. He brought his bloodshot eyes toward the ceiling, squinted, no doubt trying to surmise the new person in his living nightmare. On every job previous, Crank showed no empathy, no sympathy for the person in the chair. These people were a means to an end. A quick three hundred bucks from Seth. If he saw them on the street afterward, he barely recognized them. He'd corrected women beaters before, turned their faces into Elephant Man cosplay. The kid in the chair, now, however, didn't strike him as a typical woman beater. He resembled the sort of simp who went around berating other people for uttering the slightest criticisms of women. Like he had the word misogynist locked and loaded, ready to go the moment another man joked about shoe shopping.

But weren't the ones who admonished the loudest just compensating for their own failings? Like preachers or politicians who chastised homosexuals and ended up getting caught in public restrooms tapping their toes.

No, no. We don't know anything about this guy.

Seth said, "This chump's a noodle. Let's not waste any more time."

The chump wept louder. He said, "I don't know what you guys think I did, but I didn't...I didn't do it, whatever you think I did..."

"You familiar with a girl named Ariel? Works at the Starbucks in Hammond?" Seth spoke with his cigarillo jammed between his teeth.

"Of course..." The chump clamped his mouth shut.

Seth nodded to Crank. "Girl's brother says the girl can barely speak. Lost three molars to this chump's brittle little knuckles."

That should have been it. Crank should have taken a step back and brought Betsy in for a crash landing on the joints holding the chump's jaw to his skull. Should have turned half his mug into a fleshy purple haze. Betsy slid a bit on his fingers. He closed his fist tighter, as though that would produce the motivation to crush cartilage in the chump's nose. Everything from the tips of his fingers to his elbow felt heavy, immobile. He dropped his arm and shuffled in a circle.

In snide, sniffling tones, the chump said, "I won't press charges...you walk away now..."

Holy Jesus. How long had it been since a chump tried that? Never worked before; no, the chump had nothing to do with Crank's hesitance. His conscience, once again draping itself in Yulia's sweet, if drunken, voice: How can you judge this man? Have you seen the girl in question? This Ariel? You're going by the words of others. And even if this man did abuse his girlfriend, shouldn't law enforcement take care of it?

He slammed his palms against his own head, grunting when Betsy's underside nicked his temple. "Quiet!"

Seth and the chump stared at him.

Crank drew back his fist, aimed for the bridge of the chump's nose. Nice shot between the eyes would shut him up. But he couldn't do it. Couldn't do his job. He stepped away from the chump. The disgust washing across Seth's face reminded him of

41

his father's reaction when he informed him he no longer wanted to work in the steel mill. Seth snapped his head to the side. "Hit the road."

Crank attempted to say something, to justify his behavior.

Seth waved toward the warehouse's bent doors. "Go home and get your fucking head on straight."

Not since Crank had been told senior year at Haggard High that his GPA prevented him from graduating had he taken such a shameful walk. The shame stayed with him in the car. He angled into the lot of the convenience store. The man in the wheelchair must have been off at his spot, enjoying whatever booze he'd bought with the money he'd grifted earlier. On his way to the coolers in the back of the store, a younger guy, all bones, dressed in black, wearing eyeliner, shoulder-checked him. Crank raised his hands to grab the kid and throw him through the window. The kid laughed at him and kept going. How had he known he wouldn't pulverize him? Had he worn his newfound weakness on his face?

Je-zus.

Yulia noticed the change when he entered the apartment. "Look at you," she said. All sunshine. She took the bottle he'd bought her. "Humility. I dig it." She plopped down on the couch/bed and turned on the television. "Almost like you want to join the human race."

He sat next to her. How long had it been since they'd vegged in front of the idiot box? She flipped channels. He wanted to take the remote away from her. Knew she'd land on something he wouldn't find interesting. Sure enough, she stopped at a channel dedicated to shows about rich people turning foreclosed homes into castles. The early pains of a headache blossomed across the top of his skull. He imagined his true self, beating on his brain, demanding he cease this moronic attempt to be a normal person. "Hey baby," he said, "you mind if I work on the GTO for a while?"

She shook her head, slowly. "Oh, Crank, I love this new you. So considerate." She sounded like Miss Sparks, his kindergarten teacher. She nodded toward the table with the model car and thin brushes. "Why yes, sir, I believe I can live with that."

He'd painted the hood and side panels the previous night. Now came the delicate strokes leading to the roof. He'd decided on an ivory shade. He opened the appropriate jar and dipped a fresh brush. As his hand approached the car, he noticed a twitch. He squinted, thinking that would help. The closer the brush got to the car, the more his hand shook. He imagined smudging the window with the paint, something he'd never done. "Dammit." He set the brush down and closed the paint jar.

"What's the matter?" Yulia stared at the television as she spoke. Couldn't peel her eyes off the kitchen in a house a yuppie couple had won at a police auction. Two stoves. Who the hell needed two stoves? Were they going to turn the place into a restaurant?

No, no. We're not cynical anymore.

Juh-ee-zus!

He angled back to the couch/bed, slumped next to her. No reason to ruin the GTO. Not while his body refused to accept Mr. Nice Guy. He put his arm around her and rested his head on her shoulder. She ran her fingers across his scalp. Every few minutes, she tilted the bottle to her lips.

In the morning, Crank rolled off the couch/bed when his phone rang. On the other end, Seth said, "Well, Mr. Sparkles, Bugle took some shots at the chump yesterday. Nothing special, apparently, nothing that made an impact."

Crank pinched the bridge of his nose. His headache had improved in an unpleasant way. Pounded his temples. And not in synch.

Seth continued, "The chump made his way to Hammond last night and strangled his girlfriend. Waited for her at Starbucks. Forced her in his car, drove her to Lake Arthur, crushed her throat, and rolled her into the water. Pigs fished her out early this morning."

Jesus.

"Cops got him?"

"Nope," said Seth. "The girl's brother is furious. Wants his money back. I told him we'd eighty-six the chump. On the house. Got word he's hiding in Dyer, waiting on the Cardinal to take him south. We'll be by in ten to pick you up."

"I don't..." He didn't know what to say. "That's not my..."

"You got us into this shit," said Seth. "You get to make things right."

Crank kissed Yulia on her neck. She'd passed out on the floor, her arms and legs twisted and flailing in four different directions. She stirred, swatted him away from her. He stumbled into the bathroom and looked at himself in the mirror over the sink. He tried smiling. Loathed what he saw.

Seth refused to roll down his window in the Buick. "Smoke bothers you?" He looked at Crank through the rearview. He took a hefty puff off his cigarillo, turned his head, and exhaled in Crank's face. Crank should have shoved his head through the windshield.

He said, "Can we stop off at the Family Express?"

"The hell for?"

Bugle said, "That's a good idea. I ain't done breakfast yet."

"Make it quick." Seth turned onto 9th Street and weaved through traffic to the convenience store. He pulled into the parking lot and idled in front of the man in the wheelchair.

The grifter stared at Crank and grinned.

"Get your dumb ass in the store and get whatever it is you need." Seth finally rolled down his window.

As Crank stepped around the car, the man in the wheelchair chuckled. "You going to be consistent, big guy," he said, "or you think tossing a nickel my way one time will hold your conscience for the rest of your days?"

Crank stopped walking. Something washed over his body. Relief. Like his blood had been deprived of essential nutrients and they flooded him in one smooth movement from his head to his feet. His temples stopped throbbing. He returned the grifter's grin. "I apologize." He approached the man in the wheelchair. "I really wasn't myself yesterday."

The man in the wheelchair stretched out his hand. Must have expected another paper bill.

"No, no, no." Crank laughed. "You've caught me on a Jesus-type of day. Not Jesus, the empathetic healer. Jesus, the reborn." He grabbed the grifter by his dirty collar and yanked him to his feet. The man stumbled into the parking lot and landed on the hood of the Buick.

Seth honked twice and leaned out the window. "What the hell, Crank!"

Crank Baxter picked up the empty wheelchair and carried it to the sidewalk, near a row of rubber trash bins. He raised the chair with one hand and slammed it to the concrete. The grifter protested. Sounded just like the chump in the warehouse, the one who'd, apparently, used Crank's charity to murder his girlfriend. This encouraged Crank. He smashed the wheelchair into its individual pieces and placed them in one of the bins. He smacked

45

his hands together and entered the convenience store as Bugle stepped out.

"The hell's wrong with you?" said Bugle.

"Not a damn thing." Crank Baxter headed for the coolers. The few people standing in the aisle scattered from his path.

(2019)

THE BAG GIRL

Her supervisor, working the express lane, summoned her. "Bag girl," he said. He snapped his fingers. She wondered if he even knew her name, if he'd ever bothered to read the plastic tag pinned to her black apron.

But she hustled over. Tough to get a job in Haggard these days. Especially for a high school dropout with nothing to offer but a smile and quick hands. She grabbed a paper sack from a stack at the end of the second conveyor belt and loaded the customer's groceries. The customer slid his card into the credit machine and typed his secret code. Her supervisor asked him, "You want big bills, or little bills?"

"Twenties'll be fine," said the customer.

Her supervisor counted out five and handed them over, along with the receipt. The customer took his eggs and bananas. He didn't hide his effort to peek into the bag girl's button-down dress shirt underneath her apron. She grinned, played along. She eased her hand into her back pocket and worked the keypad on an ancient Blackberry phone: Bears jersey, khakis, boat shoes, douchenozzle.

The next customer's wardrobe must have come off the bargain rack at Walmart—a T-shirt with a bald eagle on it flying over the words DON'T TELL ME HOW TO FREEDOM and grease-stained jeans tucked into cowboy boots. On his hip, he wore a holster and handgun, just like those QAnon dorks on television. When he spoke, he barely moved his thin lips, like being civil to another human being demanded too much. She asked him if he wanted his six-pack in a bag.

"Do your job," he said to her.

She stuffed the beer into a paper sack and handed it to him as he walked by her. He didn't look at her, didn't ogle her cleavage. No matter. For the moment, the man meant nothing. He'd paid for his Budweiser with coins he'd dropped from a coffee can cradled under his arm.

Time crawled while she whipped groceries into bags and said, "Have a nice day," like a robot. The automatic doors to her right opened and the guy in the Bears jersey stumbled into the store, holding his blood-stained hands to the side of his head. He spilled into two rows of shopping carts, fell on his knees and wept.

Her supervisor scratched at a Cuba-shaped meth scab on his forearm. He said, "Dammit, not again!"

Her boyfriend used the money to score a baggie of Vikes. They each popped two and plopped down in front of his old-fashioned, humpbacked television. The news talked about the hits at the Strack & Van grocery store. Three nights over the last two weeks. She'd only been with her boyfriend a month when he'd come up with the plan. He'd found prepaid Blackberry phones at a Family Express outside of Pawpaw Grove. "This routine won't last long," he'd said. "Soon as the pigs catch on, we crack the phones and ditch them in Lake Arthur."

The first time they'd tried the scam, she'd doubted they'd pull it off. If her boyfriend got caught, she decided she'd slip the phone into a customer's bag when they weren't looking. But things went smoothly. Several customers shrieked from the parking lot. The cops showed. Then an ambulance and a fire truck. All for a normal guy who'd taken two shots to the face from a solid steel meat tenderizer. Yes, it cracked his skull a little but, you know, so what? He had money. She and her boyfriend didn't. Her boyfriend had been stealthy, moved in from behind the security cameras, dressed in black, wearing a ski mask. He smacked the guy twice with the metal mallet, reached into his back pocket, and ripped out his wallet. He'd been gone before anyone noticed the normal guy slumped over, bleeding onto the trunk of a cream-colored BMW.

That night, they'd celebrated. Big time. Seth Short sold them some Oxy and they crushed and snorted it. Everything went fine until they tried to have sex. Her boyfriend's penis lay still, like a bored slug. She said, "That's all right, I understand." For whatever reason, this infuriated him. He punched the wall and shouted at his crotch:

"You piece of shit!"

She suspected he'd meant to cuss at her. The wall, probably, a stand-in.

They stretched the first guy's money for almost a week. Then they had to pull another hit. Similar target: clean haircut, wedding ring, golf shirt, square face, smug expression of superiority when he glanced down the bag girl's shirt as he took his groceries. She didn't feel bad when he collapsed on the sidewalk, just outside the store.

The haul from the second guy didn't match the first. They tried to make the pills last as long as possible. As the baggie emptied, her boyfriend's temper blossomed. She did her best to get him going in bed. He must have been on dope a lot longer than her. His junk refused to respond. She only wanted to help. He finally shoved her to the floor and called her a bitch. "You see the fucker won't stand, don't you?" Like it was her fault.

The news report suggested the Lake County sheriff's department would establish a task force to catch the Supermarket Bandit, a name decided upon by the normal people of Haggard. She said to her boyfriend, "This is getting serious." She suggested they take it easy for a while.

"That makes no sense," said her boyfriend. He grabbed her hair and jerked her head toward him. "I need you to think," he said. "Don't get goofy on me."

She said, "I don't want to do it anymore."

At this, her boyfriend's pockmarked face stilled. "You walk away, I'll rat out the both of us."

She understood, then, her inability to plan ahead formed the foundation of all her problems in life. In high school, she'd partied and screwed around, as opposed to staying at home and studying like normal people; the ones who now lived in houses, had children, new cars, mortgages, all the things normal people were supposed to have. When she'd started using pills every day, her conscience told her it might not be a good idea. She'd tried to quit, once. No way she'd go through that hell again—walls closing in, like the trash-compactor scene in that stupid Star Wars movie normal people gushed on about. One of the boys she'd bagged in high school had, despite his good looks, been on the chess team. He explained to her how chess and life were the same. He said, "Every move you make, you must consider every possible counter. If you don't, you're dead."

* * *

The bag girl and her boyfriend gobbled the Vikes over the next four days. Then her boyfriend told her, "We're going to need to borrow some more money tonight."

She attempted, once again, to convince him it might not be a good idea. "They got cop cars prowling by every five minutes," she said. "At least twice an hour, the pigs park in front of the store, get out, and stroll through the parking lot. It's totally uncool." Of course, she'd said the same thing every night since the task force had been created.

"I think we can get away with it," he said. "You just send me customers. If shit looks cool, I'll take care of business. If not, I'll hang back and wait for your next message."

"I really don't think it's smart," she said.

Her boyfriend's chest, covered in half-finished tattoos, heaved to an exaggerated rhythm. He looked like a man about to speak his final words. "Is this going to get ugly?" His hands transformed into fists, his giant, pointed knuckles doing what his penis couldn't— standing firm. Something in his neck creaked and popped as he turned to face her. The bridge of his nose wrinkled.

She said his name. She said, "Please don't make me…"

Before she finished, he grabbed her hair and twisted her sideways. His free hand, still closed in a tight, shaking fist, hovered over her. "Bitch," he said, his chapped lips pursed like the redneck in the store with the gun on his belt, "I'm tired of you thinking you got some kind of choice."

She wished she could have summoned the strength of the gods right then and blasted her boyfriend in the mouth. The more she resisted, the tighter he gripped her. His other arm trembled, as though building steam. She didn't want him to know he'd scared her. She said, in halting, choking words, "Okay, okay…"

When her boyfriend let her go, she said she needed to get ready for work. She'd been with jerks before, but none of them had anything on her, not like this one. How long would she go away for? Would she be able to score dope in prison? What sort of awful shit would the bad girls in jail make her do for a fix? She ducked into the shower and wept as she ran a paper-thin piece of soap over her body. She lathered up the rest of the soap and used it to wash her hair. She tried dressing in the bathroom, alone. Her boyfriend insisted on keeping the door open. He leaned against the wall and stared at her. She wiped steam from the mirror above the sink with the cardboard tube from a dead roll of toilet paper. She spoke to her boyfriend through the mirror. She said, "What?"

He didn't say anything, just bored into her with his half-open, bloodshot eyes.

Friday night. Normal people came into the store angling for fresh money from their bank accounts. Almost every other customer opted for cash when they ran their debit cards. Eighty bucks here, a hundred there, over and over. She offered her boyfriend one sacrificial yuppie after another. None returned with a bloodied face and empty pockets. Every time she glanced outside the giant window at the front of the store, a squad car either rolled by in the street or crept through the lot.

On her break, she squatted near empty fruit crates behind the store and smoked a cigarette. One of her coworkers, a crumbling meth junkie who resembled a straggler from Dawn of the Dead, talked on his cell phone. He finished his conversation and went back inside. From the shadows between spotlights mounted on the roof of the store, her boyfriend snaked up and hissed at her. "How about sending me something when the place isn't crawling with pigs?"

She shrugged. "What am I supposed to do?"

He wrapped his crooked fingers around the top of her button-down shirt. She dropped her generic cigarette as he hoisted her to a standing position. "You think you can survive an empty night?" He didn't let her speak. "We both know the answer."

Maybe she sneered at him. Whatever look came across her face, it compelled him to tap her cheek with his monster knuckles. He said, "I'll make this simple for you. You pay close attention to the lot and give me a goddamn customer when things are obviously cool. You take care of this real soon, or I'm going to call the cops and tell them I saw the bag girl texting someone before the last hit."

This stunned her worse than the back of his hand. She said, "I'm on it. I promise."

Closing time approached and she still hadn't found a good prospect in conjunction with a cop-free parking lot. Plenty of normal people asked for money, like they hadn't seen the news, like they didn't know what could be waiting for them outside. She wondered whether her boyfriend would be bold enough to march into the store and confront her. She imagined him pacing the alley separating the store and the nightclub behind it. Maybe he'd punched the nightclub's brick wall a few times. Or maybe he'd used the meat tenderizer to chip away at it, thinking about the horror of sweating through the night without a fix.

Around eleven-thirty, a normal guy in one of those musclehead shirts, the kind with ornate writing nobody could read, swiped his card and collected a stack of ten-dollar bills. Hardly any cars in the parking lot. No cops anywhere. The bag girl reached into her pocket, ready to text. Then she heard coins, rattling in a coffee can. The man with the gun on his belt counted out change for a six-pack three aisles down. He'd worn his weapon again. His Walmart T-shirt this time said I LOVES ME SOME 2ND AMENDMENT! The bag girl made sure she described the man's cowboy boots and his dirty jeans as she texted her boyfriend.

The next customer in her line, a normal woman in a tank top and shorts showing off her perfect, bruise-free thighs, told her to keep her yogurt and celery separate. The bag girl said, "Sure thing, ma'am." Five pops, like firecrackers, erupted outside. She didn't even turn her head as everyone else in the store, including the normal woman, craned to see what had happened. The bag girl dropped the Blackberry phone into the normal woman's paper sack, right next to her yogurt. As the normal woman passed, refusing to make eye contact with her, the bag girl said, "Have a wonderful evening."

(2018)

DESTROYERS

You heard about Brian Klein, right? No? Sweet Jesus, boy learned himself a lesson. I know, I know, how's it possible he learned anything, freeloading in his mama's basement? Just mooching off her like a parasite. No accountability for nothing. No job. Well, shoot, what you expect? Brian's got a bachelor's and a master's in English. How you going to study the language everyone already speaks by nature and expect to have any skills worth a damn? Yes, yes, he could dump coffee in a mug, like Shirley Baker's girl LaDonna does, over there at the café on Seventh Street. But Haggard ain't Chicago, and, well, we just don't need that many English majors to serve drinks in the morning.

But don't let me get sidewise on this here story. Not this soon. So, Brian Klein's livelihood, if you could call it such, involved tracking down culprits on the Twitter and Facebook that don't sit right with the finger-wagging crowd. Brian likes to look into folks who've been celebrated for various deeds and find out if they got any dirt lingering under their toenails. For instance, Brian was one of the first to blab about Mayor Koski's flirtation with marijuana back in the 1980s, when the mayor was a student up there at fancy Northwestern. Wouldn't have bothered folks too much had Koski not gone on the tube a week earlier and claimed Hoosiers were too stupid to handle legalized weed. Much of a point as he might have had, that picture Brian uncovered, the one of an eighteen-year-old Steve Koski smoking a joint at a Dead show in Cleveland, well, it rendered the mayor a hypocrite. This society we've fashioned since the Internet became king, shoot, we just love to ridicule anyone for any possible wrongdoing. Don't much matter that Steve Koski's looking down the barrel of fifty and, having several decades between now and his college days, may have changed his mind once or twice on moral issues. Brian found some dirt on him, slung it like a cow paddy, and called it a major revelation. I suppose you might christen this the Age of the Lazy Inquisition. I doubt Brian Klein climbed out of his pajamas before making his way across his mama's basement floor, traveling from his bed to his computer, before doing a search or two on Google and finding that picture of our idiot mayor.

But here I go again, started in one direction and veering off in another. Bear with me, my friends. We got time, might as well use it. So, Brian, as always, is spending his day surfing the Internet, checking up on all the hot news stories, you know, things people talk about for three minutes before the next headline comes along. He sees this bit about an ancient football hero from Lublin named Cory Bunker. That's right, old Bonks. Surely you all remember how he took Lublin to State back in '90. Lost to them rich boys from Indy. Well, Bonks used to have serious control issues. Like a lot of young men playing linebacker for an Indiana high school, knowing full well they weren't good enough for a scholarship, even to a crappy MAC school like Ball State, and sure not good enough to ever play in the pros. They get used to the crowds on Friday nights, egging them on to flatten running backs and cripple wide receivers.

Then the glory's over. Pretty girls don't throw themselves at them no more. Carl Fork stops giving them discounts at the Napa store. These boys wind up pumping gas or selling used cars. If they're lucky, they get a construction gig that twists their spines and puts a fair amount of cash in their pockets. Bonks, he took a job sweeping up the stadium at Valpo, cutting the grass, getting it ready for games on Saturday. In the winters, he mopped floors in the lecture halls and scrubbed the bleachers and the hardwood in the basketball arena. Married that chunky Joyner girl from Pawpaw Grove. She squeezed out a couple of sons who got into the pain pills when they were teens and died before they hit twenty. Mind you, when we get to the part where Brian Klein stuck his nose in Bonks' business, note how Brian didn't pay no mind to these particular ills in Bonks' tragic biography.

Well, Bonks was driving home one evening. He sees some youngster, a sixth grader named Peyton Sipes, getting pushed around by a flock of older boys. They'd knocked Peyton off his Schwinn, if that's what the kids are riding these days, and they'd ripped his backpack off his shoulders and tossed his schoolbooks all around him like a mini-Stonehenge. They were closing in like hyenas, getting ready to damage him physical-wise. Bonks pulls over. Gets out of his '96 Chevelle, the brown one with a floor so rusted his wife's got to keep her legs up or she'll be shuffling her feet like she's in a Flintstones-mobile. He shoves that squeaky, stubborn car door out of his way and rushes over to Peyton and the bullies. It don't take him three seconds to scatter those older boys in every direction. Just showed them that fist of his that used to punish the best tailbacks in the state and growled a line or two about bashing in their skulls.

Now, it so happens a little girl named Tina Bunting had her cellphone out and decided to film the whole thing for prosperity's sake. She puts her little documentary on Instagram and, wouldn't you know it, millions of people pass it around. Goes viral, as fellows who look like lumberjacks but work in bookstores like to say. Next thing Bonks knows, he's being interviewed by all them big news outlets. Fancy reporters put microphones in front of Bonks' face and ask him how it feels to be a hero. Well, Bonks, being a humble type from Lake County, he blushes and insists it weren't nothing any ordinary, decent human being wouldn't have done. But it don't stop there. Greg Bickle, yes, yes, Greg Bickle, the quarterback for the Chicago Bears, he gives old Bonks a call and asks if he wants to sit in a corporate box at Soldier Field the next time them filthy Packers roll through. Victor Pacheco, yes, *the* Victor Pacheco, the guy who plays Astroman in them comic book movies, he sends Bonks a personal twit, or tweet, or whatever the hell it's called, on Twitter, letting him know how all them rich folks in Hollywood think Bonks is just as peachy as grape-flavored cocaine. Point being, that little gesture by Bonks, taking time out of his miserable life to make sure Peyton Sipes didn't get his ribs kicked in by a stink of cowards, that smidgeon of kindness made Bonks a celebrity for the customary five minutes the Internet grants us lowly working folk who don't live in L.A. or New York. If you read the various reports, the initial reports, that is, of what Bonks had to say throughout all this, you'll see it never inflated his head. I guess playing high school football in Indiana taught him all the consequences of taking the flattery of a mob too serious. And his time in the spotlight would have ended just like that, on a nice, positive note, were it not for Betty Klein's mooching adult son whose college degrees made him so damn incompetent he can't even secure a job putting potato chips on the shelf at the local Walmart.

You see, Brian Klein hates himself. That's the only diagnosis I can conjure that explains why he does what he does. Why he did what he did. And when a man hates himself, well, he can't stand to see another man's life made decent, even if it's just for a flash, a moment of time so insignificant, it would have been forgotten the very next week. Folks like Brian Klein, they sense beauty in this world, and their first inclination is to destroy it.

Brian Klein got to work on figuring out every Lego brick that had put together Bonks' life, leading right up to the day Bonks bullied them bullies who tried to bully Peyton Sipes. He dialed up his account at Transparency dot com, that site that finds every bit of info ever documented about another human being. Real nosy enterprise, you ask me. Didn't take Brian long to stumble across that incident between Bonks and Mel Spivey. If you don't recall it right off the top of your head, don't beat yourself up. Most folks let it drift and drown in the past since Bonks did his time and demonstrated, public-wise, his remorse for setting Mel Spivey's nose a hair to the left. You remember now, don't you? The Old Oaken Bucket, 1990. Bonks grew up in a house worshiping the Boilermakers. Didn't much matter that neither Bonks' dad nor his granddad had attended college, let alone Purdue. They'd developed a cult-like attachment to the football team and, as such, were obliged to loathe and despise the, generally, woeful Indiana Hoosiers. Except, of course, the Hoosiers came up to Lafayette that year and whooped the Boilers, 28-14. In the parking lot, after the game, Bonks bumped into Mel Spivey, who'd worn his crimson-and-white gear and couldn't help but say something to him. What kind of lousy squad loses to the Hoosiers? he'd said, grinning that goofy, toothless grin he'd earned mouthing off to Drew Richards at prom, senior year. Why the hell anyone from Lake County would root for IU is beyond me, but, you know, Mel always did his own thing. Guess that's how he ended up running the mortuary on Fourth Street. Well, Bonks, he didn't take to getting razzed right after seeing the Boilermakers lose. He brings that brick-sized fist of his back and lands it at a perfect angle, collapsing Mel Spivey's nose to the side, like folding a page in a book. Blood spills all over, so much a hot-dog vendor nearby used an entire package of napkins helping Mel get it under control. They wheeled Mel Spivey to the emergency room at St. Francis and, later that night, Mel gave a statement to the police and agreed to press charges. Bonks pleaded guilty and served a two-month sentence plus probation. He paid his debt in the form of community service, changing diapers at the Rosehill retirement community. Like I said, folks would have forgotten the whole thing, except maybe Mel Spivey, who's reminded of it every time he looks at his gangly, bony face in the mirror. It just so happens Mel's cousin Bernice worked for the *Journal & Courier*, and he convinced her to write a teeny-tiny little story about it, way back in 1990, that appeared on the last page of a Tuesday edition, next to the obituaries.

Brian Klein found that article. He found the police report, the arrest record, and the court documents. He couldn't log on to Twitter fast enough to post what he considered the truth about Cory "Bonks" Bunker. He twittered, or tweeted, or whatever the hell you folks call it, that Bonks was, in fact, a bully himself. The big corporate-controlled news outlets, ever eager to match the self-righteous indignation trickling down the average Twitter feed, picked up the story. Outlets that hadn't even reported the first part, the part about Bonks being a hero, ran with Brian Klein's correction, painting Bonks as the meanest sonofabitch who ever came up in Lake County, or Indiana, or the Midwest, or America itself. The twittiots of the land allowed Brian Klein to alter their previous impression of Bonks, to turn admiration into hatred. Them celebrities, soft enough in the brain to let an invisible mob influence them, rescinded their nice offers. All over a parking lot ruckus from thirty years ago.

Unfortunately for Brian Klein, the torch-and-pitchfork chorus on Twitter had enough influence to convince the useless bureaucrats at Valpo to fire Bonks. The very last thing that man needed in this economy, in this brutal, stupid, disgusting world we've created. His wife don't work no more on account of her foot getting run over by a forklift at Liberty Steel. The hell they going to do now? Bonks figured, best thing for him would be free room and board.

Well now, after all that, we can get to the crux of the story, the meat of the matter, if you will. Brian Klein, he heard a knock at his mother's front door just about a week ago. No doubt he'd been basking in the glory of bringing down another, in his mind, corrupt human being, someone whose life had carried just a little more weight than his. He had to compose himself, put on some decent clothes over his pajamas, and make that rough trek up them creaky, wooden steps in his mama's basement. He opens the door and, wouldn't you know it, there's Cory Bunker, Bonks, onetime hero, permanent goat, just smirking. He couldn't have asked for a more convenient solution. He said, You Brian Klein? Now, I'd just about pay anything to be able to get in a time machine and have a front-row seat, watching Brian Klein soil his pajamas. He stuttered and stammered, apparently tried to lie, say he was someone else. So Bonks tells him, I seen your picture on your Facebook page. I know who you are.

Brian started cussing Bonks in that gibberish you only hear on college campuses, calling him a reactionary, telling him all about his privilege, calling him an oppressor, if you can believe it. Bonks, he just grabs Brian Klein by that scraggly, disgusting lumberjack beard of his, yanks him closer, winds up, and lands that monster fist on the side of Brian Klein's face. Neighbors claimed they could hear Brian's jaw crack from inside their homes. Bonks rearranged his entire skull. Bent his face in like that painting of that guy screaming on a bridge. Then he turned right around and went to Haggard PD to confess. Word I've heard is he plans on representing himself in court, thinks it's the best way to get himself a nice cozy cell down in Pendleton.

As for Brian Klein, neighbors said he ain't made one move toward finding himself a job so he can detach from his mother's generous nipple. They did, however, rejoice the morning they watched him wheel his computer desk, complete with the computer on top of it, out to the trash bin in the alley behind his mother's house. Maybe, just maybe, without the Internet giving Brian Klein crumbs of glory, he might start thinking the way humans is supposed to think. He might start looking for beauty in the real world and, perhaps, upon finding it, he just may choose to leave it be.

(2018)

THE RADICAL
MR. BOGATA

Mr. Bogata told Armen Faulk to put on his seatbelt. He said, "This is where we drop the hammer." He'd passed the black SUV with Life Moments Photography written in red cursive letters on the driver-side door. The woman behind the wheel had glanced over, her forehead wrinkled, no doubt confused. Considering the icy roads, she'd been cruising as fast as anyone could reasonably expect.

At least, that's what Armen imagined the woman had been thinking.

Mr. Bogata spun his cherry Dodge Dart a hundred and eighty degrees and stopped. He put his left foot on the brake and revved the engine with his right. "Just look at her." He flipped his Spandau Ballet bangs over his ear. "Just bathing in privilege while you fucking starve."

Armen hadn't considered it in such terms. He needed to pay Lake County Gas and Electric or they'd shut off the heat in his apartment. His wife had just given birth to their first child, Shona.

When he'd explained the situation to Mr. Bogata at work, asked if Mr. Bogata's dad could give him an advance on his salary, Mr. Bogata babbled about proletariats and the bourgeoisie. He'd said, "Ain't that like this shitty, messed-up world?" He'd been marching through the aisles at his father's cement factory, making sure nobody goofed off. "Early funds from the old man? No can do," he said. "But I'll tell you what we can do." And that's when he made the proposal. Armen hadn't been too keen, but he went along, fueled by the threat of his family freezing to death.

"You sure she'll cave?" he said to Mr. Bogata as he buckled his seatbelt. The Dart barely had miles on it. Should have kept him safe. But maybe, just maybe, the woman in the SUV might be stubborn.

"She ain't got what I got." Mr. Bogata pounded his chest and put the car in drive. He flipped his bangs again. His shampoo filled the air with flowery, chemical odors. Ice beneath the wheels scattered as he released the brakes. Banks of snow created by a county plow narrowed the road to one lane. Beyond mini-mountain ranges lining the slick pavement, sugar-coated treetops hinted at the depths of the ravines on both sides. "Better hold on to something," said Mr. Bogata.

The woman craned over her steering wheel. She slapped the horn several times. She did not slow down.

Mr. Bogata stomped the gas pedal. The needle on the speedometer approached sixty. Armen's pale knuckles clutched the oh shit! handle above his door. "Maybe I can take a loan from the bank," he said, hoping Mr. Bogata would abort the mission.

Mr. Bogata parroted dialogue from Fight Club, dime-store Buddhist bullshit about living in the moment, and leaned back. His grip on the steering wheel reminded Armen of the old Maxell print ad of a guy holding onto a couch as though it were a roller coaster. Sammy Hagar or some other gaudy radio rock from the 1980s would have completed the scene. Mr. Bogata's iPhone, plugged into the car stereo, however, played nothing but monorhythmic electronica. "Besides," he said, "what bank's going to draw up a loan for a few hundred bucks?"

As they approached the SUV and the driver of the SUV refused to budge, Armen said, "How about you loan me the money, bro?"

"Bro?" Mr. Bogata sneered. "I'm your fucking boss. Don't forget that."

The woman driving the SUV snapped her steering wheel to the side. The oversized station wagon spun onto two wheels and flipped over an embankment. Mr. Bogata slowed and turned around. He brought the car to a stop at a cavity the SUV had punched through the wall of snow. "I'll chew off my left nut if that broad's in any condition to stop us now." He got out and started down the side of the ravine.

Armen felt nauseous. Even when Mr. Bogata had suggested the Life Moments photographer could solve his problems, Armen hadn't believed they'd go through with it. Mr. Bogata explained his sister Eva had revealed underclass pictures were scheduled for Haggard High that day. Mr. Bogata said the photographer collected cash only. "She'll have four, maybe five hundred dollars," he'd said. "We can split it. You can pay your stupid bill and take your wife to a Bears game or something." Armen argued with him, initially. Mr. Bogata reminded him of their time in high school—"You used to sell weed for me, remember?"

Armen had had nothing to do with drugs since senior year. For whatever reason, however, his manager bringing up their former business relationship compelled him to go along with the plan. Didn't seem so serious, anyway. Mr. Bogata described the Life Moments photographer as a bourgeois fat cat stealing money from poor parents and students in exchange for a phony memento, a flimsy piece of nostalgia designed, as he stated it, "to dupe folks into thinking their lives have more meaning than they actually do."

After Armen agreed to participate, Mr. Bogata dropped more politics. He called it a complete lack of fairness that a woman driving a fancy SUV should go home with an envelope full of money and no problems on her shoulders. "Privileged whore," he'd said, sitting in the Dart, across the street from Haggard High, watching the pear-shaped woman load ten crates of lights and camera equipment into the SUV by herself. When she walked around the driver's side, she cradled a yellow envelope under her arm, clutched it as though it contained a map to the Holy Grail. The holes in her shoes and the frayed ends of her pants legs suggested membership in the struggling class.

Armen got out of the Dart and followed Mr. Bogata into the ravine. The SUV rested, upside down, across a frozen creek. Steam rose around it, no doubt the result of different, colliding temperatures. The woman must not have worn her seat belt. She'd been tossed through the windshield and landed, limbs crooked, a few feet from the ice. Armen said, "We need to call an ambulance."

"Are you stupid?" Mr. Bogata didn't look at him when he spoke.

"We can call anonymous."

"Don't be so naïve." Mr. Bogata squatted by the SUV. He cleared broken class from the ceiling and rummaged through a stack of papers. He found the envelope and stood. As he stuffed it inside his jacket, he said, "Sweet."

The woman rolled over and screamed. Her chest heaved in rapid bursts, stopping and starting, her respiratory system an engine refusing to fire. Armen recognized her then. He'd seen her several times at Goodwill, going through racks of clothes, just like his wife did any time they had an extra nickel or two at the end of the month.

"She's gone." Mr. Bogata headed up the embankment, toward the road.

Armen stared at the company logo on the door of the SUV, crumpled from the accident. He wondered what kind of car the woman actually owned.

Mr. Bogata started the Dart and honked the horn. As Armen climbed over the embankment, Mr. Bogata rolled down the passenger-side window. "Let's motor, bro!"

Armen got into the car. He struggled with his seatbelt. His hands wouldn't stop shaking. Maybe his instincts were wrong. Maybe Mr. Bogata had been correct. Maybe the woman had been wealthy. Maybe she stood on her feet for eight hours, wrangling snotty teenagers, tolerating fussy parents out of boredom. She'd inherited millions of dollars and decided she wanted to wallow with the doomed. But he knew no such reality existed. To drown nagging voices in his mind, he spoke: "You count the money?"

"What's it matter?"

"I still need to pay the heat bill."

"Yeah, yeah." Mr. Bogata shuffled through songs on his iPhone, landed on another dance tune. Sounded like all the others. "Let's head back to my place, play some Madden."

A headache lingered near the top of Armen's brain, threatened to drape itself across the front of his skull. "I have to get home, bro…" He stopped himself. "Mr. Bogata, I mean," he said. "I have to get home, give my wife some time off."

"Yeah, yeah," said Mr. Bogata. "Relax. You just made some easy money. Like the old days, you dig?"

Selling weed in high school had *not* been easy. Even then, Mr. Bogata insisted on being called Mr. Bogata, as opposed to his first name, Howard. He once revealed to Armen he thought Howard made him sound like an overweight retired guy in a fishing cap and Hawaiian shirt. He'd float Armen an ounce of pot and expect him to sell it within a day. If Armen couldn't move the entire stash, Mr. Bogata charged interest. Just when Armen had gotten fed up with the arrangement, just when he'd decided to tell Mr. Bogata he quit, the school turned Third Reich. Haggard PD brought in Nazi dogs to sniff lockers. Sure enough, they smelled dope he'd hidden behind his chemistry book. The school's new administration wanted to look tough, so they kicked him out. He had to finish online and go through life with a GED instead of a full-fledged high school diploma. Had Mr. Bogata ever apologized for that? Admitted to some culpability? No. And when Mr. Bogata suggested he could get him a job at the cement factory, he promised there'd be no hoops to jump through. That didn't stop Mr. Bogata's dad from grilling Armen in the interview, insisting he submit to a urine test every six weeks. Had Armen not met and married Larissa Farmer, he might have gone bonkers and morphed into one of those psychopaths who expressed anger with an assault rifle. Now he had a daughter, and that daughter had, until that very moment, anchored him to sanity.

"All right." He knew Mr. Bogata wouldn't split the money with him if he didn't give him a chance to clobber him in Madden a few times. He sat back and pretended the steady thumping from the speakers in the Dart's doors didn't exist. He imagined listening to something less repetitive, like folk music from the old country, stuff his grandpa used to play on records at Christmastime.

Mr. Bogata's bedroom in his father's house was bigger than Armen's apartment. Posters of Mao, Che Guevara, and several MMA fighters covered the walls. Mr. Bogata had connected his Xbox to an LCD projector. They sat on a couch beneath it. "Here you go." Mr. Bogata handed him a controller with a loose left knob. He fired up Madden and chose the Patriots.

Armen went with the Bears, knowing full well they were terrible and he'd watch the computer version of Tom Brady throw one pass after another to streaking receivers the Bears' defensive backs couldn't compete with. On several occasions, he claimed the offensive line had gotten away with blatant holding. Mr. Bogata called him a hater and suggested Armen select a better team the next time they played.

"My family have always been Bears fans," said Armen. "I'm not going to change my allegiance just because they're going through hard times."

Mr. Bogata insisted Armen indulge a best-of-three series with him and made him endure a third contest despite having won the first two by blowouts. The sun outside Mr. Bogata's picture windows faded. Armen said, "I got to get home, give my wife a rest."

"That's cool." Mr. Bogata shut off the Xbox and started for his bedroom door.

"Can we split the money?" said Armen.

"Jesus!" Mr. Bogata nodded like a bobblehead doll. "Money's not the most important thing in life," he said. "You ever think about people in third-world shitholes? How tough they got it?" He snapped his fingers at him like a dog. "Let's go." He looked like Armen's father had the day Armen got kicked out of Haggard High for possession of marijuana.

In the car, cruising through downtown Haggard, Armen looked over at Mr. Bogata, trying to formulate a diplomatic way to ask exactly when the money would be divided. Red lights from Dairy Queen and the Princess movie theater glowed on freshly fallen snow.

Mr. Bogata snapped at him. "What?" he said. "What is it?"

"I don't mean to be rude," said Armen. "I just think we should split up the cash. I mean, a woman died, probably, I mean, just so I can pay my heat bill…"

"Money, money, money." Mr. Bogata shook his head with a pained grimace, reminded Armen of yappers on political news channels feigning outrage at something their ideological opponents had posted on Twitter. "All right, you greedy son of a bitch." Mr. Bogata turned the steering wheel hard and pulled onto a gravel road leading to Baco Bridge, a trestle across Lake Arthur adorned with the letters B, A, C, O, and S by the town's stoners in the mid-1980s. He stopped the car, got out, and trudged onto the train tracks.

Armen stumbled through the snow after him, wishing he had the guts to grab the envelope and run. He joined Mr. Bogata at the middle of the trestle.

"Your materialism is poisonous." Mr. Bogata took the envelope from his jacket pocket and thumbed through the stack of money inside it. "The best thing I can do for you, I think, is teach you to worry about more important things." Then he turned the envelope over and dumped its contents. Individual bills fluttered to the lake below like dying birds.

Armen thought of diving after them. The freezing water would probably kill him. His feet sank into gravel between the railroad ties. His body chilled as an early evening wind reminded him people were waiting on him, depending on him.

(2018)

NASTY HABITS

The records inside the jukebox in Tilly's hadn't been changed in thirty years. Maybe more. Bob Seger, .38 Special, and so on. The Doobie Brothers admonished a fool's beliefs when the suit entered the bar. The sun hadn't set outside and it spread across the floor as the door opened, interrupting the comfortable gloom Mitch Polk sunk into after his second shot of Cuervo. He couldn't afford more than booze and it barely scratched the itch to disappear from himself.

Glenn, the bartender, a mohawked tattoo artist who often spoke of a perfect idea materializing and saving his life, listened to the suit and shrugged. The suit scanned the joint, winced at a group of guys dressed in too much leather, and looked at Mitch twice. Strangers didn't single out Mitch unless they were junkies as well. And he expected nothing else when the suit sat on the bar stool next to him and said, "Know where I can get the good stuff?"

Had Mitch been modern American status quo, he would have lectured the suit about assumptions and generalizations and labels. He would have played victim, demanded to know what part of his ragged outfit—his hole-ridden shoes, his open, black button-down shirt with the elbows missing, his barely legible Molly Hatchet T-shirt—marked him. But he had no time for bullshit. Playing victim appeased middle-class boredom. He hadn't been a member of their club since his youth when his well-meaning parents kicked him out after finding a half ounce of weed in his backpack. He said, "How good?"

The suit held an open palm at the same height as the top of his barstool. He nodded and licked his lips.

"Got no idea what you're getting at," said Mitch. "I mean, to me, good stuff is a handful of Oxy, a corner of tar. If we're talking really, really good stuff, then we're talking opium, the source, you know what I'm saying? You usually don't find that in Indiana. Somebody tells you they got opium, stash it in your shower. It's probably soap." He'd stopped fretting over saying incriminating things to strangers a long time ago. Cops couldn't bust you for talking. And, frankly, cops weren't dumb enough to send in a narc in a sky-blue jacket and pants from the Men's Wearhouse. No, this guy walked in straight off Nub Street. Square as a box of crackers. As with most yuppies, he had some nasty habit festering under his skin, like a colony of maggots squirming to get to the surface.

"No, no, no." The suit leaned closer, looked around, as though right then he'd felt the need to worry about the others in the bar. "The little ones," he said. "I want to fuck a little one."

"Midgets?"

The suit grimaced. "I thought this place was…cool?" He tugged the flaps of his jacket.

Mitch said, "Place is fine. Maybe I'm not cool."

The suit put his mouth just outside Mitch's left ear. "Kids. I heard I could find anything I need here. I'm at a convention in Merrillville and I need a release. Bad."

A toucher. Lower than a chunk of petrified dogshit loitering between Satan's toes. Mitch prided himself on not judging the freaks of the world. But the pedos, he couldn't adjust his tolerance enough to see things from their point of view. His baby sister Stephanie had been ruined by a toucher. Every woman he'd dated when he still had a sex drive had been victims of touchers when they grew up. Seemed to be an entire army of these button-downed perverts roaming the country, murdering as much innocence as possible. He considered the toucher's pudgy face, his thick square glasses. He'd heard once that touchers had been victimized as children themselves, that the whole thing represented a giant wheel unable to stop turning. At the very least, the guy might help him get a baggie for the night. He said, "I know somebody."

Relief settled across the toucher's face. In an odd way, he didn't seem so different from any other kind of junkie. "Of course, I'll pay you a finder's fee," he said. He told him his name—Hector. Said he'd checked into the Omni in Merrillville for a toy dealers' conference. Mitch asked if he meant adult toys. The toucher said, "No, no. Kid's toys. Real toys. Normal toys." He said he'd flown into Chicago from St. Paul. "You ever been to the Twin Cities?" He spent five minutes babbling about the weather in Minnesota. Just small talk, same thing all junkies did when they believed they'd reached the end of their grueling search and wanted to translate their gratitude in the form of a phony dialogue, a false promise of friendship. No big deal. Once Mitch got what he needed, he'd never deal with the pervert again.

"Let me make a call," he said to the toucher. He slipped off the bar stool and rounded the corner leading to a lone bathroom with no door. A hooker named Rose, famous in Lake County for having removable plastic teeth, sat on the ringless toilet sucking off Randy Fort, a speed pusher who'd no doubt negotiated a swap with her. Rose waved to Mitch with a free hand and he waved back. He picked up the receiver on a payphone attached to the wall. The instructions on how to deposit coins and dial had faded to gibberish. It was one of the last payphones in Lublin and, hence, explained why junkies and prostitutes of all ilk populated Tilly's. He dialed Seth Short's number and rested against 1980s concert posters on the wall as he waited for someone to answer.

The toucher insisted Mitch sit on newspapers in the passenger seat. He said he'd rented the car, said he'd gotten a combo deal on the Internet for his flight, lodging, and transportation. The interior smelled like the toucher, like spoiled cheese. "Company's paying," he said. "They offer to put up our wives and children on these trips. For obvious reasons, I leave mine in Minnesota. Wouldn't be good for them to know about Daddy's hobbies."

Mitch sighed. "I can see that." He remembered something his father once told him—Mitch, his father had said, sometimes when you get home at night, you just got to wash your hands. His father had sold insurance for Agra. His father never got hooked on anything illegal. He came home every night and gulped half a fifth of Jim Beam before dinner. At the table, he'd ask Mitch, What'd you do today? Mitch could never figure out what that question really meant. If he didn't respond properly, his dad would take him to the living room and tell him to lay across a wooden coffee table between the couch and television. His dad used a long-handled shoehorn to beat him. The ongoing romance with pain in his lower spine started and sustained Mitch's need to self-medicate. In high school, friends assured him weed would do the trick. But it didn't. And when he found himself living in a crash house near Haggard, no longer interested in school or maintaining the middle class lifestyle his parents and baby sister enjoyed, he began gobbling pills and worked his way to heroin.

"Turn here," he said to the toucher.

The toucher said, "Here?" He scratched his chin, looked confused.

"This guy," said Mitch, "this guy who's going to help us, he lives out here. Trust me. This is the kind of stuff you hide from the nubs, the regular folks. Folks like your neighbors, I'm guessing."

"Of course." The toucher nodded. His face turned red. "I don't want you to think I'm an amateur."

Mitch laughed. "Oh, I don't think that about you, Hector. No, sir. Not that."

The road blended from pavement into gravel. The rental car wobbled between empty cornfields. On rolling hills in the distance, electric windmills rotated. Mitch considered the compromise he'd made, the rationalization that abuse existed on a never-ending cycle, and that touchers, ultimately, had to be forgiven since, according to psychobabblers, they'd been touched themselves as children. A younger version of Mitch would have argued free will demanded a sensible victim of molestation make damn sure he or she didn't turn around as an adult and do the same horrible thing. His own slavery to dope, however, eliminated his belief in free will. He remembered going home for Thanksgiving just a few years earlier. His sister, recently turned twenty-one, revealed a smarmy fuck named Beau Blix snuck into her cabin at summer camp, ten years before; She'd woken up with her Cookie Monster covers removed and her panties sliding down her legs. She'd frozen still, unable to comprehend this living nightmare. She'd heard Beau Blix, then seventeen, hiss into her ear, "This never happened." When Mitch asked where he might find Beau Blix now, his sister said, "It's cool. Someone slashed his throat at the Motel Dee-Light on County Road 81." She said Beau Blix had met a male prostitute there and gotten robbed and killed. Another fucking yuppie on the downlow. Goddamn nubs. Mitch had felt guilty, like he should have known something had gone wrong when his sister returned from camp that summer and switched out her modest wardrobe for shorts that cupped her ass cheeks and tank tops barely concealing her boobs. But he'd been a full-time stoner by that point. His sole concern? Finding and consuming drugs. Even at the expense of watching out for his baby sister.

Pointing at a series of rundown barns and a farmhouse to the left, Mitch said, "There you go."

Again, the toucher donned a pained expression. His face scrunched, like he'd eaten a fresh dog turd. "You sure?"

"Just pull through the gates." Mitch regretted not being able to talk with the toucher, maybe Dr. Phil him into revealing what had turned him into a pervert. Then again, Mitch had read on the Internet how rich people liked to fuck children because, in their bizarre concept of reality, money allowed them to do whatever they pleased. He didn't want to hear a story about the toucher going to a masked ball and getting introduced to his hobby by some wealthy monsters who hadn't even been victimized as children themselves.

The toucher listened as Mitch directed him to a jumble of cars, some new, some old, scattered across dead land behind the farmhouse. Smoke spiraled from a crooked chimney on the roof. The toucher seemed more relaxed as he parked the rental and got out. "Nice place," he said.

Mitch knocked on the back door and Bonnie Short answered. When she didn't sell dope with her man Seth, she taught at a preschool in Pawpaw Grove. She stood on her heels to peer over Mitch's shoulders. She got a peek at the toucher and settled her feet on the floor again. "This him?" she said, as though maybe Mitch had brought more than one person.

He pushed into the house, forcing her to step aside. "Seth around?"

"'Course he is." She brushed at her lilac, dandelion-patterned skirt, like she'd been offended by something.

The toucher remained outside. He held his hands in front of his crotch. He'd squeezed his knuckles white. "Name's Hector. May I enter?"

Bonnie straightened her face and said, "Of course, sugar. Come on in out of that autumn cool. We got a fire going and everything."

Mitch walked through the kitchen. Mildew permeated the air. Dishes had been stacked in both sinks so high they'd spilled onto the counter. In the dining room, Seth Short sat in a chair, its legs held in place with duct tape. On a round table next to him, a pile of baggie corners filled with tar beckoned Mitch like a siren. "Hey," he said to Seth.

Tying a baggie corner together and placing it with the others, Seth licked his fingers and stood. "Mitch." He towered over him, his gaunt head nearly scraping the ceiling. He wiped his fingers through a bushy mustache he'd cultivated since Obama's first administration. "You bring the guy?"

The toucher stepped into the room. He offered a hand to Seth. "Name's Hector," he said. "From Minnesota. You ever go there?"

Seth smirked. "No need for foreplay," he said to the toucher. "I recognize a man in need when I see one." He moved behind the toucher and put his hand, bigger than a catcher's mitt, onto the toucher's neck, wrapped his fingers around it. The toucher shot Mitch a glance, wore the expression any man does when he realizes he's at the mercy of someone physically more powerful. Seth turned him and aimed him for a closed door. "Everything you need is right here." Before he moved the toucher any further, he lifted the back of the toucher's suit jacket and tore out the pants pocket occupied by the toucher's wallet. The toucher tried to protest. Seth must have tightened his grip on his neck. "Hush now." He flipped the wallet open with one hand. "Nice haul," he said to Mitch. He tossed him the toucher's wallet. Still addressing him, he said, "Have

Bonnie set you up." Then he used his free hand to twist the knob on the door before him and the toucher.

In the other room, Cory Bunker, a former Haggard High linebacker who'd gone bonkers from too many concussions, and Bugle Stork, who'd gotten his name on account of his nostrils being as big as the mouth of a trumpet, stood on either side of a fireplace, each holding rusted plumbing wrenches. The toucher jammed his feet into the hardwood floor. His polished dress shoes produced no resistance. Seth slid him into the next room and threw him into the stone façade surrounding the fireplace. The toucher smacked his forehead and dropped to the ground. Seth followed him in and shut the door. The toucher squealed, maybe trying to scream. Mitch heard the clank of one of the plumbing pipes collide with the toucher's flesh.

Bonnie stood at the table. She shuffled through the baggie corners. "Don't you fret none, sugar." She separated several of the bigger corners from the stack. "You're doing God's work, far as we're concerned." She nodded to the chair wrapped in duct tape. "Have a seat." She disappeared into the kitchen for a moment and returned with a box of fresh needles. "Stole these from CVS." She cooked one of the corners on a dirty spoon. After pulling the dope through cotton and into a syringe, she handed it across the table to Mitch. "Seth says the first one's on the house."

"I get to keep the toucher's wallet?"

"Of course, sugar," she said. "Incidentals are yours." She sniffled and started fixing another needle. This one, Mitch assumed, for herself. Or maybe her husband, or the boys, for when they finished their work. She said, "Money we'll get scrapping that fancy car of his, I'm sure it'll run similar to whatever cash he's hauling."

"Guess so." Mitch rolled up his frayed pants legs and looked for a vein on his calf. He jammed the needle in, no longer bothered

78

with tourniquets or any other ritualistic crap novice junkies wasted time on. The dope trickled down the back of his head and suggested the table might be soft as a pillow. As he nodded closer to it, he heard the toucher in the other room. Sounded like he had to force his words through a mouthful of blood and jagged teeth. The toucher made some sort of promise, swore he'd change his ways. The clinking and clanking from the plumping wrenches bashing in the toucher's bones drowned his gargled voice. Soon there was only silence, sweet silence, then the music of angels, somewhere in the corroding alleys of Mitch Polk's conscience, singing hymns to the prospect of the toucher's money holding him over for another day or two.

(2018)

THE BUNKER GIRL

Gilbert's mother sat on the couch with him. She wore her usual baggy sky-blue muumuu and a clear shower cap. They'd been watching Family Feud when the old-fashioned flip model in Gilbert's pocket chirped like a parakeet. He palmed it and answered. As Seth Short gave him instructions, Gilbert's mother tapped his elbow, repeated, "Where'd you get that?" She pointed at the cell. Would not let Gilbert focus on the conversation with Seth. He said, "Hold up, boss," and put his hand over the mic.

"You know I can't multitask," he said to his mother.

"I want to know where you got that."

Gilbert stood and started for the front door. His mother said, "You ain't working for them rednecks again, are you?"

He stepped onto the stoop outside and slammed the door. That would let her know to mind her own business. "I'm back," he said into the phone.

"Stink," said Seth, "how'd you like to drive a car to Chicago for me?"

* * *

Seth lived in a two-story shithole near Lublin. What lawn remained hadn't been mowed in a quarter-century. Rot plagued the farmhouse's cedar walls. Termites, Gilbert assumed. Smoke lolled over the edges of a leaning chimney. Seth lumbered like Lurch from The Addams Family. He walked Gilbert around to the side. Slipped him the keys to a maroon Honda Civic. Nothing flashy, nothing to catch the beady eyes of Lake County or Chitown pigs. He punched an address into the car's GPS and said, "You ask for Diego when you get there." He explained how to hide the package in the trunk, underneath the factory-provided spare tire and flimsy jack. "Stink," he said, "I'm glad you're with us again." He waved a finger in his face. "I want New Stink on this job, not Old Stink, you dig?"

Gilbert told him he could count on him. Promised he wouldn't fuck things up. Seth sent him on his own. A relief. He'd gotten in good with him once more by accompanying Crank Baxter on a hit the previous week. A nasty task. Hadn't slept well since. Crank picked him up in a rusted Ford Courier. It coughed and choked as he urged it to fifty miles an hour. They pulled into Haggard after midnight. Parked across from the underground bunker at the water plant. Crank Baxter resembled a World War II tank. Squat, sturdy frame built in the mills in Gary. He stalked the bunker's green haze hunched over like a cat poised to kill. Shoved his way through clusters of junkies. He grabbed people by their throats, lifted them off the ground, and Darth Vader'd them about a guy named Bobby Arnold. A young woman with honey-brown hair directed them to a concrete lip above the sewage ducts. Rodents nipped at Bobby Arnold's toes as he scrunched himself inside the narrow space. Must have figured it an easier fate than dealing with Crank Baxter. Mud stained his jeans and trendy Johnny Cash T-shirt, the one with the Man in Black showing the camera his middle finger.

Crank dragged him through the crowd. The junkies cussed, threatened to kick his ass. "Help me get this piece of shit to the surface," he said to Gilbert. For a junkie, Bobby Arnold looked healthy. Overweight. Youthful, shiny skin. Probably new to the scene. Gilbert struggled to keep his balance as he pushed Bobby's feet through the steel-rimmed portal leading to the sane world. Crank hoisted him from above, his monster hands clutching the junkie's shoulders. As Gilbert climbed the iron rungs to the street, Crank Baxter thwacked Bobby Arnold in the side of his neck. The junkie collapsed. Crank dragged him by his ankle to the truck. "Let's go, Stink," he said. Gilbert wished he had the balls to correct the gangsters, tell them nobody needed to call him Stinky anymore. His underarms and unwashed Hanes begged to differ. He helped Crank chuck the junkie onto the bed of the pickup. Two five-gallon gas canisters and several coils of chains had been secured behind the cab.

As they bounced and slid over a gravel road near Pawpaw Grove, Gilbert asked, "What's the deal?"

Crank stared at him for a moment. "Bobby's been busted seven times now and never once been tossed over the wall."

Gilbert ceased thinking of Bobby Arnold as a junkie. Junkies deserved sympathy. Rats? They required swift execution.

"Going to take him for a ride." Crank steered the Ford onto a wide, dirt path at Pawpaw Hollow. He brought the truck to a halt among cedars and birch trees. "Let's get the snitch prepped for his last meal." He clarified: "Bobby's going to feast on twigs and pebbles before meeting his maker."

They secured the rat's legs to the chains and attached the other ends to a hitch on the tail of the truck. Bobby stirred as they set him on the ground. "Why not just shoot him?" said Gilbert.

"Boy needs to think about his mistakes as he's dying." Crank walked back to the cab.

Bobby Arnold opened his eyes. He held his pudgy hands out to Gilbert. Baby hands. "Please, buddy…"

"Stink!" Crank honked the horn twice.

The engine growled. An impatient predator. Crank jammed his left foot onto the brake pedal and fed the engine gas with his right. The hood rattled. He released the brake and the truck coughed before taking off.

Not even the chorus of the wind harmonizing with the Ford's raspy protests drowned the horrid sounds of Bobby Arnold's shrieks. Fate must have blessed him, snapped his neck early in the ride. Gilbert glanced at his sideview mirror. The rat's limp body trampolined off the earth like a fish reeled across a lake. The image visited him any time he caught a moment's sleep the following days.

Crank slowed and stopped the truck in a clearing. He pointed at a parked, violet Geo. "Our chariot home." He directed Gilbert to reach under his seat. Said he'd find two sets of work gloves. "This is going to be messy."

The road repurposed Bobby Arnold into a sopping crimson slab. As they heaved the dead rat onto the bed of the truck, his skeleton collapsed. Multiple bones must have splintered or broken. Crank instructed Gilbert to climb over the fleshy glob and retrieve the canisters of gasoline. Gilbert handed them to him. "Jump down now," said Crank. He picked up one of the canisters and splashed the corpse. He nodded to the other canister. "Let's go, Stink. This heap ain't going to bathe itself."

Gilbert unscrewed the lid. The canister felt heavier as he doused the front end of the truck. He circled the vehicle several times. The air wobbled like a movie flashback, reeked of benzene. Crank threw his cannister onto the bed and told Gilbert to do the same. He produced a Zippo with a copper Grim Reaper etched into the side of it. "Stand back, Stink." He lit the Reaper and aimed it at the Ford. Sparks jumped until a small fire danced where the

Zippo landed. The flames mated with the fuel. A vicious gust preceded a blaze encompassing the truck and the rat.

Crank smacked Gilbert in the chest with the back of his hand. "Let's go, Stink." He threw a set of keys at him and walked toward the Geo. "You drive this time, buddy."

A week later, Gilbert exited the Dan Ryan Express at 35th and crawled through cramped traffic to Union. The GPS directed him to a two-story brick building on the corner. A liquor store occupied the first floor. Men on the sidewalk asked for spare change from anyone entering or leaving the booze shop. Women in painted-on skirts chirped at him, asked if he needed some pussy. One woman, could not have been older than sixteen, offered to suck his dick. He patted his pockets, pretended he had no cash. He found the entryway leading to the apartments. On a keypad with scratched-off numbers, he dialed the number Seth gave him. A man on the other end asked what the hell he wanted. "Name's Gilbert," he said. "I'm here to see Diego." The door buzzed and he ascended a set of marble stairs riddled with cracks. At the top of the steps, a man wider than Gilbert, dressed in safari shorts and a wine-red Bermuda shirt, chomped a cigar. His snow-white eyebrows and hair suggested he had a decade on Gilbert.

In a polite tone, he said, "Please raise your arms." He patted down Gilbert with one hand. A lazy inspection. "It's cool," he said. "Seth tells me you are old school."

Gilbert pointed to the gray patch of hair arcing over his left ear. "Been around a while, amigo."

"Si, ese." The man appeared neither amused nor impressed. He directed him into a small room with torn furniture and a flat-screen television mounted in the window. He rested his cigar across the top of a Coke can. From under a couch suitable for a museum— the ornate, wooden arms and legs carved to resemble the feet and claws of an unidentified animal—the man produced a briefcase with a broken combination lock. He opened it and pointed to a collection of plastic baggies stuffed with pills.

After closing the briefcase, the man stepped aside. "All yours."

Gilbert left the apartment. He recognized several of the pills—Vikes, Oxy, and Fen, ready to be crushed and snorted or shot into the arms of Lake County's living dead. He never plugged dope. Considered it a waste. Better to pop a pill, let the body warm to the chemical seasoning. A couple of Vikes, he could haunt a bar and not make a fool of himself in front of women. Then again, he hadn't gone out in years. He preferred to sit on the couch in his mother's house and veg to late night television.

He roamed the liquor store. Pulled an RC from a cooler near the emergency exit. As he approached the counter, he noticed a young woman in cut-off shorts. Ass cheeks peeking out the bottom. Pink halter top. No bra. Honey-brown hair. His attention volleyed between her and the clerk as he paid for the soda. He told the clerk to keep the change.

He ignored the men outside asking for money, the hookers ogling him, as though he owed them attention. The young woman in cutoffs trailed him to the rental. He stopped and said, "Excuse me?"

"I know you." She placed her knuckles on her hips. A nearby streetlamp, one of the few working on the block, washed out her eyes. "Met you in the bunker, in Haggard."

He ducked into a shadow.

"Last week," she said, "you barged through looking for that fat ugly snitch, Bobby Arnold."

"No idea what you're talking about."

She waved her hand. "Oh, don't worry none. Nobody's going to miss that fucking skinhead."

"I got to go." Gilbert started for the driver's side.

"Back to Haggard?"

Gilbert pressed the button on the keychain to open the door.

"Think I could get a ride?" The young woman tilted her head. "Really," she said, "I promise I won't tell no one you clipped the snitch."

"Who said I did?"

The young woman stepped toward the passenger-side door and fiddled with the handle. "Come on, man," she said. "I don't get a ride, I'm going to have to spend the night with a creep. You know how dudes from Chicago are. Total douchebags."

Gilbert's lungs deflated. He'd yet to shake the moronic belief that doing favors for women led to sex. Sex he wouldn't pay for in the most overt, socially unacceptable manner. He imagined the young woman in lingerie, after a shower and a makeover. She'd look good. What had she been doing in the bunker? No blemishes on her arms or legs from plugging dope. Did she pop pills? He could buy some from Seth and ask the young woman to chill with him. "Hop on in." He clicked the trunk button on the keychain and wedged the briefcase between the spare tire and first-aid kit.

As Chicago's obscene skyscrapers diminished in the rearview, the young woman unloaded biographical details. Whether she told the truth, Gilbert didn't care. She claimed a redneck shot her ex-boyfriend in the Van & Strack parking lot. Cops wanted to pin it on her. Not enough evidence. She laid low in the bunker to be safe. "Never know when the pigs might decide to take a closer look." Gilbert asked if the man's death had been her fault. She changed the subject—"Got a line to Classy Companions."

"What's that?"

"Escort service."

"Oh."

"I won't be selling my pussy, per se. Just showing it to douchebags while they tug themselves." She stared out her window. "I know, it's kind of gross. But I won't cross that line. I won't take money to let a man inside me."

"You shouldn't," said Gilbert. "I mean, I'm not judging. I just think…You look like you have more respect for yourself, you know?" His mother would have laughed. She'd put her foot down a year ago, told him to stop bringing hookers to his bedroom.

A purple and gray sky loitered over the dead mills in Gary. The young woman mumbled. Something like "Yeah, sure."

Gilbert took the first exit to Haggard. He needed to gas up the rental and grab something sweet for his belly. He pulled into the Shell station overlooking I-65 like a parent at a playground. He asked the young woman if she needed anything. She said no. Very considerate of her. "Sit tight," he said. He swiped his mother's credit card at the pump and fed the tank. He greeted a posse of homeless cats he'd gotten to know in recent months. They stood by the door, opening it for customers coming and going, hoping for charity. "Get you on my way out," he said to them. He perused the snack aisle, his mouth watering at the shelf of Hostess sugar bombs. He nabbed a cherry pie and stood in line. He used his own cash. On his way back to the car, he dropped three quarters in the smudged free hand of the man holding the door. The guy sneered. "It's all I got," said Gilbert.

Guilt from not helping the homeless man buy a four-course meal and whatever poison put him on the street evaporated when he returned to the rental. The woman had taken off. Jesus, he should have known better. Good looking twentysomething, even if she dwelled in the bunker, what the hell would she want with a rotting fifty-three-year-old? He grinned at himself in the rearview as he settled in the car. Half his teeth missing. Blackened, chipped, crooked. A hillbilly Redd Foxx. "Loser," he said to himself. He took off and cruised to Seth's place. The big man sat at a crumbling picnic table out front. Flaking paint suggested the benches had once been canary and the table itself, burnt orange. Probably stolen from the long-condemned Haggard public swimming pool. Gilbert parked and meandered to the table, wiping pie crumbs off the corners of his mouth. Seth picked up the barrel of a black revolver he'd disassembled and peered through it. "What's the word, Stink?"

Gilbert clicked the keychain and popped the trunk. "No issues." He walked with Seth to the car. Seth arrived a second earlier. His eyes rummaged the trunk.

"Johnnies pulled you over," he said, "looks like you'd a had nothing to worry about."

Gilbert's throat dried. The young woman had robbed him. He'd fucked up. Again. He marched around to the driver's side, bent down to examine several buttons near the emergency brake. "Shit…"

"Where's my product, Stink?" Impatience colored Seth's voice.

The young woman had found the button for the trunk, no doubt took a peek, and snatched the briefcase. He inhaled. Closed his eyes. "I guess…there was an issue."

Seth slammed the trunk and circled the car. "How's that?"

"I gave a ride…"

Pointing at him with the detached gun barrel, Seth said, "Changed my mind, Stink. Not in the mood to hear the story. Get me my pills or get your affairs in order. I'm tired of giving you second chances."

Technically, he'd only given him two second chances. Gilbert stuffed himself into the car and started it up without saying anything. Seth approached the driver's side and tapped the window with the gun barrel. Gilbert rolled it down. The big man leaned in and said, "Got one hour, Stink. Beyond that, I'm sending Crank Baxter your way. You know how that's going to turn out, don't you?"

* * *

Gilbert's mother dubbed Seth Short The Overseer. Said he'd have taken delight in whipping returned runaways back in the day. Gilbert considered these things as he climbed down the rusted rungs to the bunker at the water plant. Usual litter of junkies on the narrow lip beside the flowing sewage. They'd slumped against the concrete wall, huddled, on the nod. Shit. Common sense told him he'd retrieve nothing. Perhaps he could offer up the young woman as a sacrifice to Seth.

"Anybody seen…" He'd never thought to ask her name. Or did she tell him and he'd forgotten? Yes, yes. She said it once. Something fancy, something foreign sounding, like she belonged in a Hans Christian Andersen story. A junkie in a striped shirt and torn blue jeans raised his head. He squinted, as though staring into the sun.

"Sup, dawg?"

"I'm looking for a girl," said Gilbert. "Short shorts, pink halter top, dusty brown hair. Possibly blonde. I'm not good with colors."

"Think you mean Cym." The junkie used his bulbous forehead to point down the line. "She's earned a spot with Mitch."

"Mitch Polk?" said Gilbert.

The junkie said, "Last names are still a thing in the world upstairs?"

Gilbert thanked him and walked into the tunnel. Mitch Polk had been a runner for Seth. Gilbert heard he'd died at some point. Overdosed. Or Seth had him eighty-sixed. Depended on who told the story. The bunker hid a lot of Haggard's dirt. His eyes adjusted to the dim and he spotted the young woman's legs, draped over another man in filthy jeans. "Hey," he said when he reached her.

The young woman took her time facing him.

"What'd you do with it?" he said.

The man she'd wrapped herself around forced his chin higher. "Who are you?"

"Mitch?"

"Stink?"

"Nobody calls me that no more." He returned his attention to the young woman. "I need the shit you peeled."

"No idea what you're talking about." The young woman flashed her teeth. So white they glowed in the dark. A flirtatious smile. No doubt certain she could tease her way out of trouble.

"Ain't here to bullshit," said Gilbert. "I just need that shit back."

Mitch must have thought Gilbert couldn't hear him. "He talking about the dope?"

The young woman played dumb.

"Oh, bro," said Mitch, "that shit's long gone." He waved his hand back and forth. "Everybody got some." He clutched the brick wall to help him get to his feet. "And thank you, if you're the donor."

Gilbert's fingers clasped the junkie's clammy throat. "You understand Seth Short's going to turn your ass inside-out, right?"

Mitch laughed. "Wouldn't be the first time."

"Dude," said the young woman, "the shit's gone. Just deal with it."

Gilbert released Mitch, let him drop to his knees to catch his breath. To the young woman, he said, "You familiar with karma?"

"That's superstitious shit for people who can't handle reality."

"It's very real," said Gilbert.

The young woman shrugged.

The bunker's emerald glow tapered. Gilbert knew he could pick her up, throttle her, throw her into the river of sewage. Wouldn't matter. He'd still have to go to Seth empty. Still have to take his lumps. "Okay," he said to the young woman. "See you on the other side."

He climbed out of the bunker and drove to the Family Express on Seventh Street. He used his mother's credit card to buy a bottle of Night Train and sat in the rental downing it. Before putting the Honda into gear and heading toward Seth's, toward whatever harsh judgment The Overseer had in store for him, he called his mother on the disposable flip phone. "Hey," he said. "Just wanted to thank you." She asked what the hell had gotten into him. "You jet through life," he said to her, "someone right next to you, telling you what you need to hear, and you don't listen until it's too late."

"Well, yeah…" Her sarcasm? *Music.*

"I got to go, Mom." He coasted onto Seventh Street. He fired up the rental's satellite radio. Found a station playing songs from the nineties. All that grunge crap he couldn't stand, taking him back to his days as a young man, when he still believed his future lay in Chicago and beyond. When he still believed he would not be buried in the same town he'd been born in.

(2021)

CYMBALINE

The men stank of beer when Raven and her partner Sparrow arrived at the suite. Yuppies, she assumed. Business types. Maybe they'd closed a deal and wanted to celebrate, spill good money on a pair of escorts. One of them disappeared into the bedroom and returned with a tawny leather briefcase filled with bundles of dope. He set it beside an old-fashioned phone on a coffee table in front of the couch. Opened it, revealed its contents. He pushed Raven's partner to plug her arm. Raven had brought Sparrow knee-deep into the bullshit. Didn't want her sloshing any further. She said to the man, "She don't do that."

The men hadn't even loosened their ties. Rigid. Like stockbrokers. Two skinny, one fat. The hefty guy introduced himself as Bobo. He pointed to a goateed colleague sitting by himself on a mauve recliner near the couch. "That there's Thing One." Then he nodded, with his chin, at the man who'd retrieved the dope. "Call him Thing Two." Fate blessed Thing Two with high cheekbones and a pointed nose. A pretty boy. Every time he spoke, every time he urged Sparrow to shoot the heroin, every time he countered Raven's protests, she fantasized driving her spiked heels through his beady eyes.

She said, "I'll plug it. Not Sparrow, though." How many times would she have to repeat herself? She reached into her gargantuan, bubble gum pink Gucci knock-off bag and pulled out a slim, cardboard box containing bleached rockets.

"Sparrow, is it?" Thing Two fished a wad of cash from his pocket. A brass clip decorated with the Eye of Horus held the money together. He flicked twenty-dollar bills in her direction. "It's not often I get to see a woman deflowered. I mean, here, I guess, it's your veins. I mean, if we're all being honest, right?" He looked at Raven, eyebrows raised. "I'll give you each a thousand dollars to strip, juice up, and lick each other dry."

Glitter flaked off Sparrow's cheeks as she shook her head. "You don't get to touch us." Raven wished the girl would stay quiet.

"Cut the shit." Thing Two rested a fist on his knee. "We look like cucks or something? I know the official line. We tip you to shake your ass. And I know for the right amount of money, you cross that line, become whores. No different than those sluts cruising Temple Boulevard."

"You need to watch your…" Raven slapped her palm across her lips. This guy, Thing Two… She hated guys like him, guys who believed they still ran the world. She caught his tell, though, as soon as she admonished him. His pigeon eyes dropped to the floor. Less than a second. Long enough to notice.

Weakness.

A real man wouldn't have flinched. And that's when she got the idea: The dope in the briefcase could fetch a fortune on the street. She knew where to unload it. She'd take Sparrow on the road with her while she figured out a new life. She'd daydreamed such opportunities. The urge to eighty-six Lake County increased when

Miss Tiffle, the stale broad running the escort service, put Sparrow in Raven's charge. She shared her goals with the girl and the girl seemed game. To catch the men off guard, however, the girl would have to lose her cherry.

"I'm sorry." She crossed the hotel's pale, plush carpet and put her hand on Thing Two's shoulder. "Sometimes I forget my place."

The man's breathing slowed. He refused eye contact. "Don't let it happen again." Probably learned the routine from his father. His grandfather. Generations of men barking at women like overseers on a plantation. He finished tossing twenties onto the floor. "Two grand, ladies. Let's go."

Raven leaned toward Sparrow's ear. "You trust me?"

The girl nodded.

"Listen, honey, I don't want you making a habit of this. You wait a week after today and go back to letting it drip into your nose. This shit ever goes into your veins again, you might as well start digging your grave."

"I thought you said…"

She winked at her. "Remember what we talked about?" She swept her hand forward, painted an imaginary horizon. "The road," she whispered.

Sparrow relaxed. Dim track lighting overhead splashed shadows around her eyes. "Really?"

Pulling her close, fondling her for the men's enjoyment, Raven said, "Follow my lead." She undressed the girl, taking time to cup her breasts after unhooking her bra, kissing her nipples until they stood. She removed the girl's panties with her teeth. She excused herself to get water in the suite's cramped kitchen. She prepared two syringes. The girl hitched a nod before Raven plucked the drained rocket from her arm. Her thin, pink lips eased into a grin.

"Oh, yeah," said Thing Two. "Like falling through the stars, all gravity and none, all at the same time, no?"

As Raven plunged the cook in the other syringe into a vein on her ankle, she stared into Sparrow's eyes. Miss Tiffle had sent her to Raven's apartment in Haggard after Raven's previous partner Shannon overdosed and, surviving, moved to Iowa to live with her parents. The girl said, "Call me Cymbaline." Raven told her it sounded lovely but too complicated for the sort of work they did. She explained the men had money, but not much in the brains department. "No, no," said the girl. "Cymbaline's my legal name." Her folks must have been hippies. To go with Raven's bird theme, she christened her Sparrow, mostly because of her long auburn hair and unblemished, porcelain skin.

Raven kissed her sparkly candy-flavored lips, brought her gently to the floor and trailed her tongue across her arms, to her hips. She slid her spiked heels off, placed them near the girl's head. As she licked Sparrow's thighs, the girl's moans oscillated between real and performed. The men's chatter morphed into animal grunts. Bobo, the heavy guy, cleared his throat. "Gentlemen..." He lumbered through the tiny doorway to the bathroom.

Raven tilted toward her spiked heels. She would plant one in each of the remaining men's crotches. She slid out from between Sparrow's legs. Smiled at Thing Two. He smirked. As Raven crouched, her hands approaching her heels, Sparrow rolled away. The girl sprang onto the coffee table, snagged the heavy house phone, and smashed it into Thing Two's face. The man's nose exploded, showered the couch with blood. Raven shook off her surprise at the girl's speed. She grabbed one of her heels and moved toward Thing One, who'd taken to his feet, his hand inside his jacket. He must have been focused on Raven. Must not have seen Sparrow's foot until it crushed his throat and sent him tumbling into the recliner. Sparrow, house phone still in hand, leapt off the coffee table and landed the phone's metal base on his forehead.

Bobo stumbled out of the restroom, gray dress pants around his ankles. "What the hell?" He sounded like a child wandering in late for dessert, discovering all the brownies eaten. Raven shoved a spiked heel into his shoulder. The big man ripped the shoe from his flesh with a stupid, confused expression. More blood. Thin streams, like a punctured waterbed. "You bitches are d…" Sparrow launched from the recliner. She swung the phone's cord around his neck and dropped to the ground, forcing him to fall with her. She jerked sideways, avoided getting smushed. She kicked him onto his belly and then, like a bull rider holding on for dear life, pulled the cord backward until the man's gargled protests filled the room with music made of gravel. Before the behemoth could buck Sparrow off him, Raven wedged her elbow in the small of his back. The man arched, allowing Sparrow to tighten her grip. Both women stayed on him until he emitted a sound Raven had only heard once—a growl, flushed down a toilet. Her father made the same noise when he died with a police officer's baton squashing his windpipe. Sparrow eased her grip. Raven put her hand on her arm.

"Hold up." She felt for the man's pulse. "He could be fooling." Satisfied the man had expired, she stood. "Gather your shit." She stepped on Thing Two's face as she closed the briefcase.

He said, "You sluts are in trouble."

Raven slipped into her heels and dug a spike into the man's ear canal. "You want to be like this fat fuck?" She directed his attention to the dead man near the bathroom.

Thing Two closed his mouth.

"That's what I thought."

* * *

They tore south on I-65. Raven pushed her rattling Toyota Starlet to ninety. The car quaked like a junkie trying to eighty-six. She glanced at Sparrow every few seconds. The girl dabbed at crusted blood on her hands with a monogrammed towel she'd swiped from the hotel. Any time she caught Raven looking at her, she laughed. "What?"

Telling her she'd surprised her in the suite would have been an insult. As though she expected her to tie her hair in pigtails and skip to school. Sparrow had decided to be an escort. She must have had some dirt under her nails. No finishing-school Barbie pursued such work unless she really, *really* hated her father. Sparrow never spoke foul about her parents. Raven speculated somewhere in puberty a cousin tugged her panties while she slept. Maybe sat by her bed and jacked off. Anything more serious, hell, she'd probably be hooking. She'd played things so innocent. Raven couldn't believe she'd fallen for it. "Nothing," she said, every time the girl questioned her.

They pulled off the highway north of Lafayette. Found a motel called the Sunset Inn. Two stories. Semis and moving trucks occupied the lot. Not quite a shithole. Beige paint on the joint's wooden slats appeared fresh, recent. The clerk, a balding man who reminded her of a hairless Dumbledore, explained what sort of tip he required to overlook her refusal to show identification. He adjusted his rainbow suspenders every time his eyes undressed Sparrow. His quizzical, uneven brows suggested he expected his wrinkled dick to perk up and he couldn't fathom why time had robbed him of the joy. "You ladies hoping to be invisible," he said, "I got no qualms. You want me to keep it to myself, well, that's an extra hundred."

Raven paid the old fart with bills she'd lifted off Thing One and Thing Two. She let Sparrow take the clip they'd pulled from the fat man's pocket. "This means the cops or anybody else comes asking, you don't know a goddamn thing." She dropped the money on the counter before the coot could touch her hand.

As the man took the cash, he said, "That's how it works."

Once inside their room, Sparrow shed her clothes on her way to the bathroom. She ran water into the tub.

Raven lounged on one of two beds covered in dusty manila sheets. She turned on the humpbacked television sitting crooked on the dresser. Found a local news broadcast. No mention of the mess they'd left in Lake County. She opened the briefcase and counted the bundles. She found her smartphone in her bag. Grinned, for a moment, at the cover image, a selfie she and Sparrow snapped the first night they gigged together. Dressed in matching wine-red lingerie, they'd twisted their lips into goofy adolescent pouts. Since leaving the suite, Sparrow seemed, well, maybe in shock. She didn't behave like someone who'd snuffed a man. Raven considered the girl might be a serial killer. All the innocence, the tenderness she'd shown since she started working for Miss Tiffle? A performance. The act of a sociopath. She dismissed the idea as paranoia. She scrolled through her contacts and dialed the man she'd been waiting to talk to since her decision to rob the yuppies.

"Yo." Syd Mustard. Former boyfriend. White boy from Glencoe. Thought he'd been born in South Central Los Angeles.

"Listen," she said, "I ran into Henry. He's obese, know what I'm saying? Like, he's Honey Boo Boo times ten. I wanted you to be the first to have a shot at, you know, procuring..."

"Yo, why don't you rent yourself a radio station and broadcast that shit all over the world?"

"I'm doing you a favor," she said.

After a pause, he said, "Where you at?"

* * *

She waited for Sparrow to finish her bath and drain the tub before taking her own shower. Syd knocked on the door while she patted her skin with a yellowed towel. Smelled like it had been soaked in mildew. She wrapped the nasty thing around her body and let him in. He'd turned thirty a year ago and still wore his Sox cap sideways and an oversized Blackhawks jersey. Sparrow had sprawled out on the other bed, giggling at a SpongeBob cartoon on the television. She pretended not to notice Syd. He pretended not to notice her. Raven pretended she couldn't read either of them. She directed Syd's attention to the opened briefcase. When he reached for a stack of bundles, she slapped his hand. "I'd put it at one, maybe two hundred grand."

"Damn, girl. Where'd you get it?"

"You want it?"

"What you asking?"

"All I want is fifty. That's fair."

"I'm a have to come back with the money."

"I figured. How long?"

He massaged his chin. "I know a boy," he said. "South side."

"Can you get it tonight?"

"Yeah, yeah." He started for the briefcase.

She held out her arm. "Excuse me?"

"I need to show them."

"They can take your word for it."

He protested.

"You the big man on campus, ain't you?" she said. "Go tell your badass friends what's up."

"You don't want none yourself?" He grinned. Another man convinced he knew more than God.

"I got fifty g's, I don't need this shit. I'll buy my own."

He shook his head. "See, now...that don't work for me. You're a junkie. Why not..."

She wrapped her fingers around his jaw and jerked him forward. "We're not playing 60 Minutes. You either want in on this, or you don't." She spun him toward the door. "You get back to me by midnight, Syd, or I'm selling it somewhere else." She shoved him out of the room. He said something she didn't hear as she slammed the door and whisked the security chain through the slot.

Sparrow said, "Who's that?"

"Loser," said Raven.

"And you're selling the shit to him?" She didn't wait for Raven's answer. "Let's do some, while we're waiting."

Raven shut the briefcase. "Might be a good time to think about quitting."

Crossing her legs, Sparrow said, "You told me quitting was the same thing as death."

"For me, yeah." Raven sat on the other bed. She rested a palm on the briefcase. "You're not..." She remembered the alter ego she'd witnessed earlier. "I mean, you haven't been lying to me about plugging it, all this time?"

Sparrow stood and displayed her pristine arms and legs. A performance appropriate for an old-fashioned department store runway. "Clean as a whistle."

"So," said Raven, "it'll be a piece of cake for you to walk." She reiterated her vision of the future, how the two of them could take the fifty grand and go anywhere. As she described a life free of drugs, free of pawing, leering perverts, she decided the girl needed to see what withdrawal looked like. She needed to see Raven clutching the walls, projectile vomiting, and cranking her clit like a fiend when her libido returned. "I'll kick, too. I'll show you my commitment."

101

Sparrow plopped down once more. "Or," she said, "we could split the money. Do our own thing."

An invisible knife stabbed Raven in her belly. She shouldn't have cared. The girl made no promises. They'd fooled around a bit, sure. She'd figured that had been for Sparrow's benefit. Her concern for her seemed more maternal than anything else. She understood what her mother must have felt like the day she told her she'd dropped out of Edison High to move to Chicago and pursue acting. "I don't think that's a good idea. Not right now."

The girl asked why.

"We don't know who those guys are."

"Douchebags," said the girl. "Yuppie douchebags, remember? You called them that twice, on the way here."

"Maybe." Raven excused herself to go into the bathroom. She turned on the hair dryer provided by the motel. Hopefully, the girl would hush. She closed the door. To go through with something so serious, they'd need each other's support. Didn't she see that? The more she thought about it, the angrier she got. She stormed into the main room. The engine on the dryer must have been louder than she figured. She had not heard the girl step outside. She followed her, saw the girl had taken her smartphone. She snagged it from her. "What the fuck?" The girl had isolated Syd's number and, apparently, intended to contact him.

"Jeez," said the girl. "Why are you so tight?"

"What were you going to say to Syd?"

She looked away.

"Excuse me?" said Raven.

The girl folded her arms across her chest. "You're not my mother, you know."

Raven bit her lip. She stared at the highway in the distance. She imagined being in one of the cars on it, racing south, already finished with this mess. In a controlled voice, she said, "Listen, we're on the run. It's not easy. It'll be a whole lot worse if we have to dodge the johnnies alone."

"Actually," said Sparrow, "splitting up will send the cops in different directions. They won't know which one of us did what." She stepped closer. "Unless, of course, one of us says something."

Raven gripped the girl's elbow and shoved her into the room. She followed her in and slammed the door. She calmed herself. Breathed slowly. "Cymbaline," she said, "I need you to trust me. We don't have anybody else."

The girl ogled the briefcase.

Raven sat on the bed with the dope. She set the briefcase on her lap. "I'll hold onto this for now."

The girl flopped onto the other bed, faced the wall. "Stupid Nazi."

Scanning the room, Raven noted everything the girl could turn into a weapon. The phone on the nightstand between the beds. The remote control, resting near the girl's shoulder. The drawers in the dresser. Maybe a maroon Gideon's Bible inside one of them.

The girl fell asleep. Not long after, Raven's smartphone chirped. The high-pitched squeal startled her, sent her over the edge of the bed. The briefcase and smartphone landed on top of her.

"Yo," Syd said on the other end. "It's like this, homie. My boy in Chitown, he tells me that shit you got, it's hotter than pussy on the moon."

"The moon is cold, Syd," said Raven.

"Nah, nah," said Syd. "It ain't no little thing, you know what I'm saying? You all took that shit from the big boys. Now, I can come get it and they'll take it back, no questions asked."

"Who the fuck do you think you are?"

"Yo, baby girl," he said, "it works one of two ways, you hear me? You give me that shit on your own, or they coming to snatch it out your dead hand, you feel me?"

She took deep, abdominal breathes. She would not break. "And if I tell you to tell them to go fuck themselves?"

"Raven, girl..."

"How about I plug all the shit at once? Nobody gets the dope. They don't get to fuck with me or my girl."

"Ain't no need for this to get federal."

She looked at the girl, now standing a few feet away from her. "And if you come here and we're gone?"

He sighed into her ear. "They'll find you. Go to Mexico, they'll find you. Shit, go all the way to Siberia and shit. They...will...find you."

"And if you come here and, say, the dope is gone, but I'm still here?"

No hesitation: "I'ma have to sell you out."

"Okay." She told him she'd wait for him.

The girl said, "What's going on?"

"Those yuppies didn't sound Russian or Italian."

"So?" The girl affected the sneer of a snotty twelve-year-old.

"I think we have to give them back their drugs."

The girl's eyes darted around the room. She lurched for the hotel phone. Raven dropped the bottom of her fist on the bridge of Sparrow's nose. The girl staggered backward and fell onto the bed. She screamed. A fearsome banshee wail. Once on her feet, she moved for the phone again. Raven slammed the briefcase into her bloodied face. The girl collapsed to the floor. Raven knelt and checked her neck, confirmed she still had a pulse. She sat on the bed. She wanted to cry, feel sorry for herself. That wouldn't solve anything, however. She could lament the lack of devotion, faith on the girl's part another time. She unwrapped a bundle from the briefcase and prepared a syringe with what looked to her like three times too much. The girl stirred as Raven plugged her arm with the deadly juice. She dumped the rest of the bundles into her clumsy, oversized knockoff Gucci bag. She would leave the empty briefcase with the girl and let Syd decide how to satisfy the big boys, whoever the hell they might be.

She gathered the rest of her stuff, got into her Toyota, and rejoined I-65. She'd emptied a rocket full of dope into her foot before heading out. Cornfields on either side of the highway glowed purple under a half-moon and clusters of stars beyond it. She'd set her smartphone on the passenger seat. It buzzed as a call came in. She cradled it in her hand, uninterested in who might be bugging her. Her eyes shifted, back and forth, between the road and the cover image on her phone's screen, the selfie she and Sparrow snapped after their first gig. A thunderstorm developed ahead of her. Roiling clouds obscured the moon and the stars. She rolled down her window and tossed the phone into the empty night.

(2020)

THE OLD
PISSING WALL

The old pissing wall? The side of a rundown, red-bricked building on Fourth Avenue once housing a wholesale vendor of cheap stuffed animals. Purple bears and yellow frogs given as prizes at carnivals and amusement parks. Years ago, Timo Vela and his buddies relieved themselves in the alley between it and an aluminum siding warehouse. In those days, they ran meth for Mr. Losa to rich gringos in Valpo and Merrillville. Most of the guys he'd worked with back then caught bullets for trying stupid shit in federal neighborhoods. Now, Timo collected on bets gamblers made with Mr. Losa. During October, football, baseball, basketball, and hockey stepped on each other's toes. The risk junkies piled debt they couldn't honor. No time to find parking at a legitimate establishment, sneak in, and hope nobody noticed him using the toilet without making a purchase. The old pissing wall would have to do. Timo had just scraped a white-haired mayate's forehead across the jagged surface of an unpainted picket fence in

Hammond and he had less than an hour to make a house call in East Chicago.

He pulled to the curb, forcing a homeless mother and her son to jump onto the sidewalk, and got out. Newspapers, fast food wrappers, cardboard boxes, and a potpourri of other garbage crunched beneath his feet. Collapsing pup tents lined crumbling storefronts. The air reeked of human waste and decay. He ducked into the alley and found a space between metal trash cans glued to the ground by petrified filth. As he unzipped and sprayed a faded Taylor Swift concert bill posted on the wall, something rustled to his right.

"The fuck?" He kicked away a sheet of crusted bubble wrap, revealing a battered young woman. She reached up, tried to speak. Blood stained her swollen, potato-shaped face. He moved more garbage away from her. She'd been dropped in the alley naked. Pink welts, bluing bruises, and crusted gashes decorated her body. Her long blonde hair had matted to her shoulder. Despite the hell she'd endured, her wide, ocean-blue eyes glowed under the Lake County sun. When her throat found air, she produced only a croak.

Timo stepped to his left and finished pissing on the wall.

He ripped west on State Road 53 in his sputtering Kia. If traffic clustered, he whipped onto the shoulder and snuck past the confusion. He zigzagged the streets of East Chicago until he arrived at a beige, one-story apartment complex on Bird Avenue. Looked like it might have housed so-called respectable middle-class families in the 1950s. Timo didn't know about the economic status of the other residents, but the hipster he'd been sent to collect from, a disinherited rich boy named Howard Bogata, barely earned the nickels necessary to pay his football debts. Timo parked out front and climbed over the wooden gate leading to a tiny, square patch of concrete behind Howard's apartment. The stench of his three undisciplined retrievers lingered beyond his sliding glass door. Timo made eye contact with him. Howard's panicked glare suggested he'd gotten a notion to run but hadn't done so in time. Timo rapped the glass with his knuckles. "Open up." His voice, in these situations, reminded him of his father, a Desert Storm veteran who'd dropped dead from a brain parasite Timo's senior year of high school. His father had not approved of the direction America veered after September 11.

"Country's soft," he'd said. "Nobody takes responsibility for their own actions. Bunch of fucking twelve-year-old girls calling themselves men."

He'd believed in corporal punishment and beat Timo any time he found dope in his room. "Don't you know this shit turns you queer?" He'd wave the baggie of grass, or pills, or powder, with one hand and use his other to sock Timo in his mouth. He often split his lip. A few times he'd blasted him hard enough to turn his nose into a faucet. Timo's mother would suggest he avoid making his father angry. Timo threatened to go to Child Protective Services, threatened to tell his teachers whose classes he barely attended. In response, his father slammed a thick PVC pipe into the side of his face. "Say some shit like that again. See what happens." He said Timo should fight his own fights. "You want to show me who's boss? Bring it. Otherwise, appreciate who puts food on the table and a roof over your head."

Timo swore he'd pay his father back. Someday. Then, in 2008, his father passed out while watching the Trojans throttle the Irish on television. Two weeks later, he checked into Kaiser Permanente. Scans never paid for showed his brain had dissolved like a clump of cauliflower in a bowl of soda pop. After Timo's father died, his mother returned to Guadalajara, leaving Timo to battle America on his own.

Howard opened the glass door. "Hey man…" The forced smile, the syrup in his voice…indicators he didn't have the money. Three bony mutts fussed over a chew toy so mangled it no longer resembled anything identifiable. Torn and faded posters of Huey P. Newton and Mao Zedong hung halfway on the walls, rolling over where tape holding the corners lost grip. The moist fragrance of unkempt dog nearly suffocated Timo. Smelled worse than the blossoming homeless colony in Lublin. He held his nose and spoke:

"Patriots lost."

"You're telling me." Howard ran his delicate fingers through a glob of unwashed gray hair framing his face and hanging past his shoulders. "They always find a way these days, don't they?" He scratched a dried chocolate stain covering an image of Mickey Mouse with a Hitler mustache on his T-shirt.

"Not my concern." Timo retrieved a small leatherbound notebook from his back pocket. He opened it to a folded page. "You thought they'd cover. They didn't." He tapped the figure next to Howard's printed name. Fifty dollars.

Howard shifted his head left and right, like the arm on a metronome. "Yeah, man," he said. "Thing is, I got to take Sully in for a checkup. I think she's got worms. Her heart's already bad, so…"

"Who the fuck is Sully?"

Howard pointed to one of the dogs. Told him the other two were called Sandy and Angel.

"Ten percent per day," said Timo. "You know this."

"Aw, man. Give a brother a break."

"You're not a brother," said Timo. "You're a guilt-laden white boy from Haggard. A pandering, condescending heir to manifest destiny. I'll be here tomorrow for the fifty-five you now owe us."

"If I don't have it today, what makes you think I'll…"

Timo shoved Howard's head into the metal frame on the glass door. Blood bubbled and spilled from his nostrils, colored his mouth and chin tomato red. "We go through this shit every time," said Timo. "Mr. Losa's had enough. Said I should crack your skull, you pull your usual weasel shit. I were you, I wouldn't worry about that stupid fucking dog. You got something in your wallet? Anything at all?"

Howard disappeared into his bathroom. He wept as he ran water over a towel and wiped off his face. Waiting for the dumbass to return, Timo watched a small television propped on a dinner tray in front of a couch with no cushions. A news broadcast cut to a couple of rural gringos. The announcer said they were from Regina, somewhere in Canada. A husband and wife, both sporting hair grayer than Howard's. They held up an airbrushed senior portrait of a porcelain blonde named Amy Hicks. Said she'd run away, gone to Chicago to be a model or something. Timo tried to convince himself the girl's wide, ocean-blue eyes were not the same he'd seen in the alley by the old pissing wall. Last thing he needed. Some conscience trip. Didn't the girl's parents understand? Your daughter flees for America, kiss her goodbye. The best thing that could happen to her? A quick, painless death. An overdose at a party attended in effort to blow a lizard for a walk-on in a fucking AT&T commercial. Maybe she hooks up with a psychopath from the Chitown suburbs. He cuts her into pieces and distributes her across I-95, like rose petals down the aisle at a wedding ceremony.

Nope.

Not his problem.

Howard emerged from the bathroom holding the soaked towel over his face. He spoke through it, his voice muffled. "I got twenty I can give you today."

"Great," said Timo. "Tomorrow, I'll come back for the other thirty-five."

* * *

The rest of the day went pretty much the same. Losers trying to negotiate their way out of either paying or taking a beating. Usually both. Timo imagined himself no different than his father, distributing pain the way a priest offered the host at church on Sundays. Don't have Mr. Losa's money? Hold still. This is going to hurt. A lot. He'd grab a chair, a butter knife, a Barbie doll, transform it into an instrument of torture. A trick he learned from Bruce Lee's book on Jeet Kwon Do—*anything can be a weapon*. When he got home, his girl Corina told him to fix a couple of cans of ravioli. She'd been in her studio, working in a Garfield T-shirt and American flag panties with FUCK TRUMP! written in sparkly letters across her gym-sculpted bubble-butt. She'd bathed in blue and yellow acrylics. Some art project involving painting lewd pictures into history textbooks she planned on presenting at an exhibition produced and attended by hipsters.

In the kitchen, Corina's transistor radio had been left on, tuned to a talk station. She enjoyed listening to conservative pundits bemoan what they called the browning of America. Code, of course, for the diminishing population of gringos who didn't know how to come when they fucked. Timo reached over to turn the dial. Days he returned home with multiple shades of blood on his knuckles, he preferred 1260, the oldies station. The innocence of early rock and roll, hiding its hormonal engine in metaphors, allowed his mind to wander to a place where Lake County looked clean, like it did in black-and-white photos from the 1950s. A place where people like him—his angry father, his negligent mother, Mr. Losa, the degenerates he collected from every day—didn't exist. He held off, however, when the uptight female DJ announced the Hicks family had offered a five-hundred-thousand-dollar reward for the return of their daughter.

Corina entered the kitchen. She'd scrubbed the paint off her hands and switched out Garfield for Hello Kitty. "They talking about that bitch from Canada?"

Timo tried not to wince. His girlfriend must have noticed him looking away. She said, "What, you give a shit?" She laughed and helped him open the second can of ravioli and dump it into a pot on the stove. "These bitches run away from home all the time, end up floating in the lake, cut to pieces in the park, strangled in that bunker in Haggard, whatever. Something happens to us, they don't talk about it on the news. Why the fuck would I care when something happens to them?"

"You're better than that," said Timo.

Her eyes walked the ceiling one time before she said, "Make my dinner."

"They're offering a lot of money. Half a million."

"For what? That bitch is probably bleeding out on a table at some Satanic rich people party in Valpo. You think you give them a corpse, they're going to pay you shit?"

"Someone they love is missing."

She shoved him aside. "You seem to think my dinner's going to make itself." She moved the pot back and forth over the flame on the stove. "Worrying about some fucking puta. Oh my God..."

"I think I know where she is."

Corina stopped working the pot. "You shitting me? You're kidding me, so help me, I'll snip your nuts off while you sleep."

"She's by the old pissing wall. I'm pretty sure."

Her face scrunched as she considered him, as though the veracity of his claim could be read somewhere on the legs of his jeans, or the clenched fist of an illustrated Darth Vader on his T-shirt. She shook her head and said, "Do not fuck with me, Timo."

* * *

They exited I-65 and crawled the streets of Lublin at the posted speed limit. They wanted no attention from the police or the scattered zombies crazy enough to wander downtown at night. Timo slowed near the old pissing wall and parked. Most of the pup tents on the sidewalk were still, their occupants snoring like machines. A drunk staggered toward them, threatened to crash into Corina. Timo pulled her out of the way. The drunk, his face layered with grime, tripped and smacked his head against metal bars protecting a store with plastic army soldiers displayed in the window.

They turned the corner into the alley between the defunct stuffed animal vendor and the aluminum-siding warehouse. An October wind rippled a mismatched carpet of newspapers and hamburger wrappers spread across the concrete. Rodents chirped warnings to their enemies. Timo put his hand in front of Corina, as though protecting her would somehow make the rodents disappear. She said, "The hell were you doing here in the first place?" He explained the pissing wall, how it served as an emergency bathroom. "Disgusting," she said.

He started to rationalize his behavior, expressing his frustration with both the traffic in Lake County and the lack of public restrooms. He stopped, however, as they stumbled upon the young woman.

A pulsating moon dropped pale, blinking light on her lifeless body. How long had she been dead? Impossible to tell. Her skin had turned gray. Her wide ocean-blue eyes, however, still commanded attention. Corina slapped her hand over her face. The stench from the woman's corpse seeped into Timo's nostrils and forced him to do the same.

"Oh my God." Corina stepped backwards.

Timo had experienced the fragrance of death before; the horrid odor stuck to the senses like a parasite. He leaned in and lifted his foot to nudge the girl, to make sure she would not move. As his sneaker hovered over her shoulder, a rat the size of a terrier poked its head from under her thigh and hissed. Blood caked its snout. It had buried its jaws in the dead woman's flesh and clearly resented the interruption.

Corina screamed and ran out of the alley. Timo followed her, unable to hurl sound from his dried throat. They booked to his tiny car, got in, and slammed the doors, as though the rat had grown a hundred times its size and pursued them. He looked in the rearview. Nothing but steam rising off the pavement and curling around tents and trash cans. Corina's chest heaved as she spoke. "Never mind. Someone else can have the money."

"We can tell them where the body is," said Timo.

"And become prime suspects?" she said. "Are you stupid?"

October blended into November. Business rolled as usual. Corina presented her installation at a warehouse near Gary. The women wore librarian glasses and severe expressions suggesting they'd never taken a relaxing shit in their lives. The men had grown wild lumberjack beards in effort, Timo suspected, to demonstrate they had *not* been collectively drained of their testosterone. They wore T-shirts adorned with pictures of Marx and Che. They clutched plastic cups filled with alcoholic punch and discussed the performance art as though they'd witnessed the Second Coming.

The news had stopped reporting on the grief of the Hicks family. No one collected the reward. No one offered a clue as to the fate of their daughter. Timo kept his mouth shut. Corina convinced him the people in charge of the world would blame him for the gringa's demise. "They'll say you killed her and lock you up." Timo had done nothing but break the law his entire life. How funny would it be to get busted for something he had nothing to do with?

The collision of sports seasons reached a stressful peak during the World Series. Timo clocked eighteen-hour days bashing skulls for Mr. Losa as the degenerates of Lake County decided the Cubs couldn't possibly break the old curse and win the pennant. The more they protested, the harder Timo beat them. He nearly put Howard Bogata in the morgue when the spineless cuckold suggested Timo get psychological counseling for what he called anger issues.

"You gutless fuck…" Timo broke the tank lid of Howard's toilet over his skull. "This is work, brother. Nothing more."

Eventually, he found himself in downtown Lublin, in a traffic jam, needing to unload the gallon of coffee he'd consumed over the morning. He inched onto Fourth Avenue and parked in a tow zone. He ducked into the alley with the old pissing wall. He had not been there since the night the rat chased Corina and him from the dead woman's body. As expected, the corpse had been moved. Or maybe devoured by rodents. Oh well. Every motherfucker for themselves. Like that guy Darwin said: Survival of the fittest.

He unzipped his pants and looked for a fresh spot on the old pissing wall. The faded Taylor Swift concert bills had been covered by HAVE YOU SEEN ME? posters. Amy Hicks' wide, ocean-blue eyes beckoned from each identical picture. He aimed at her face and let loose. Something rustled in the newspapers surrounding a cluster of trash cans to his right. Could have been a rat. Could have been a bum. Timo finished dousing the HAVE YOU SEEN ME? poster. He returned to his car without looking back to see what had been moving in the alley. He tuned the radio in his Kia to a conservative talk station and laughed as salty gringos lamented the fall of the Roman Empire.

(2018)

THE THING ABOUT PADLOCKS

Long ago, too far back for Bob Cork to remember, the word MASTER faded from the bottom of the padlock securing the gate to his chicken coop. He pondered this as he shoved the wooden frame in place and closed the lock on the latch. The blueprint he'd used to build the coop and run called for the latch and padlock without explanation. He'd assumed it prevented the chickens from escaping.

He wished the hens good night, cooed their names, and walked across his yard. He brushed brittle autumn leaves from his wife's tombstone on his way to the kitchen door. He said, "Another day, Judith." As he stomped his boots on a mat by a set of rubber trash cans, he recalled his desire, thirty years earlier, to buy a house larger than his one-story Sears model. Maybe in Merrillville. Maybe Valpo. Cancer squatted in his wife's uterus and medical bills prevented escape from Haggard. His fifties evaporated into his sixties. The cancer finished its murderous work on his wife. In a blink of time faster than lightning, his seventies arrived. The house no longer felt small. Large, in fact. Sometimes too large. He often woke in the middle of the night, rolled over, and threw his arm in the direction he expected it to land softly, arced around his wife's hips. His hand flopped on the empty space next to him and he'd remember. Dread smothered him. I'm seventy-four? Seventy-five? How much time had passed? Exactly where had his life gone? He had no children to celebrate birthdays with and he'd lost track of his own. Some nights, his heart knocked his chest as hard as he used to beat on doors and windows before kicking them in and arresting suspects. He'd get out of bed and walk the corridor between the bedroom and the living room. The walls, once so narrow, now seemed a mile apart from each other. His breathing staggered. He'd grab a framed picture of his wedding ceremony, focus on the image of Judith in her white gown and veil. "Soon, Judith," he'd say. She'd complemented her dress that day with a handcrafted necklace that day, a turquoise pendant he'd bought her on a trip they'd taken to New Mexico, back when Route 66 connected the Midwest to the Santa Monica pier. He'd left the necklace in a box of Judith's clothes he'd donated to the Salvation Army. Clothes he'd held onto for a decade in the irrational belief his wife would return home someday and require them.

He awoke that night to a thumping he believed his heartbeat until he opened his eyes and recognized the racket came from the yard. Metal on metal. Clanking, like someone doing construction work. He whipped aside a patched quilt his wife crocheted while watching the Watergate trials, forty years earlier. He threw his legs over the bed. His feet searched for his slippers. Once protected from the cold hardwood floor, he pulled down a Marlin shotgun from the top shelf on his side of the closet. He felt around the shelf for a box of shells. With the weapon loaded, he padded into the living room and peered out the window. A firefly moon winked behind meandering clouds. A slim figure crouched in front of the gate to the chicken coop. Looked to be male, though celebrities on television had taught Bob not to assume anything about anyone these days. The intruder beat on the padlock with an engineer's hammer.

Bob glanced at the wedding picture, at young Judith. "You won't believe this."

He stomped into the kitchen and picked up the receiver to a maroon rotary phone attached to the wall. Visitors always marveled—"You still have one of those?" As though his lack of a mobile phone rendered him an indecipherable relic. The emergency operator asked what he needed. She sounded like an impatient teenager at a burger joint.

"I got a trespasser," he said.

The woman clicked her tongue. She asked for his address and assured him law enforcement would soon arrive. Her tone throughout hinted at disgust. In addition to other oddball things the television preached these days, protecting one's property had become a crime itself. He'd managed to pretend such upside-down developments didn't concern him. Until this night. He opened the door to the yard and stepped out, the gun raised as he approached the intruder. "Hands where I can see them."

The slim figure tumbled to the side, losing the hammer as he scrambled to his feet. His head swiveled, no doubt considering an escape route. Bob racked the shotgun. "You're going to have to answer for this decision you've made."

The young man resembled a skeleton with scant meat and muscle on the bones. His T-shirt hung on his shoulders like a rag draped over a fence. He said something. Slang. Gibberish. Bob raised the gun higher. The young man's chest slumped. He sighed. Must have been used to this sort of confrontation. Bob motioned for him to move away from the chicken coop. He stood over the engineer's hammer. Let the young man know any attempt to retrieve it would be a mistake. The padlock lay in two pieces at the foot of the gate. "Afraid you're going to have to reimburse me for that, son."

A Lake County cruiser arrived. No lights, no sirens. Richard Sanchez got out of the vehicle. He stopped, possibly having noticed Bob, the shotgun, and the young man. He put his hand on the butt of his department-issued nine-millimeter. "Evening, Cork."

"Evening, Sanchez." Bob aimed the barrel of the shotgun toward the ground.

Richard appeared to relax as he approached the young man. He shined a small flashlight at his eyes. After they conversed in a shared vernacular, Richard searched the young man. Pulled a candy-bar wrapper and cell phone from his back pocket. He said something else to him and handed him the phone. The young man made a call, spoke to someone on the other end. Richard escorted him to the cruiser, opened the rear door, and, Bob assumed, instructed him to take a seat. Once he'd closed the door, he turned to Bob. "Eddie Reyes. His mother's on the way."

Bob scratched dried, flaking skin covering his scalp. He remembered having hair there, remembered it as though he'd gone bald five minutes ago. "You're so familiar with him," he said, "why not take him in?" His knees groaned as he squatted to snatch up the broken lock.

"Things have changed, Cork." Sanchez rested his hands on his utility belt. "Way we do things now? We let the parents take care of rascals like Eddie here."

"That boy's got to be at least twenty."

"Twenty-three, if I'm not mistaken."

"Well now, how in the world is his mother going to make a difference? Time to get that boy into shape was, shoot, last century, when he was barely out of diapers."

A coughing car engine competed with owls and crickets. A single headlight washed over Bob's street. A hatchback shrouded in blue exhaust settled behind the cruiser. The muffler blasted twice as a tiny woman huddled behind the wheel shut it off. She exited the vehicle and stalked the rear of the squad car, glaring into the window Eddie Reyes rested his head against. His eyes threatened to leap from their sockets the moment he saw the woman. The woman, not even five feet tall, rapped the cruiser's window with knuckles begging to escape scarred, stretched skin. The woman spoke the young man's slang. No mystery as to the nature of her communication. Richard called her over. To Bob, he said, "Maria. Eddie's mother."

Maria delivered hard words at a machine-gun pace to the officer. Richard donned exaggerated expressions of pain and concern. The woman then chastised Bob. A sundress hung loose on her emaciated frame. A turquois pendant decorated her neck. Bob considered asking where she'd found it. He heard Judith's voice admonish him: Don't you think she's embarrassed enough?

Richard broke his concentration. "She promises to punish the boy when she gets him home."

"Who you trying to kid, Sanchez?" Bob nudged the officer on his shoulder. "She said a whole hell of a lot more than that." He struggled to pin his focus on the conversation between the mother and officer, and not on the necklace he'd bet all he owned once belonged to his wife.

The officer nodded. "She doesn't like us doing her job for her."

Bob tried not to sigh. "You must be joking." The woman could not have been more than fifty. The lines around her eyes cut deeper than his. She returned his scrutiny. She pursed her lips and rocked her head in small, deliberate movements, up and down, up and down. So confident Bob would fold. He held out the broken lock. "Kaput," he said. He couldn't even convince himself to be angry.

121

"The thing about padlocks," said Richard, "they rarely do the job we think they're supposed to."

"Well…" Bob gathered air into his lungs, huffed his chest. Pretended, for a moment, three decades had not passed since the last time he'd proven himself in any relevant test of strength. "The kid needs to learn a lesson, you ask me."

"Come on, Cork." Richard sounded like a suspect, desperate to evade arrest. "The boy's trying to get some food in his belly. Bring a chicken home to his mother."

"How's that my problem?"

A rumble loud as a croaking bullfrog interrupted. Richard shrugged. It hadn't come from Bob's stomach. He knew the language of his body's complaints. It must have been the woman. He didn't want to look at her just then; he peered into the police car. The young man's eyes never recovered from the shock of seeing his mother. Bob took Richard aside and spoke softly. "Do me a favor, Sanchez," he said. "Haul the kid in, make him sit in a room for an hour or so." He started for the door to the kitchen. "Let the mother know what's going on. She can spring him when the hour's up."

The officer said, "No charges?"

Bob waved his hand in the air. "That's the idea." He stepped inside the house and shut the door to the growl of the woman's car. He kicked the lid on the recycling trash can near the sink and tossed the broken lock into it. "Well, Judith," he said, "looks like I'll be headed to the hardware store tomorrow for a new one." He chuckled on her behalf. She must have known, just as much he did, no such thing would happen. Not tomorrow. Not ever.

(2021)

LAST EXIT
BEFORE TOLL

"Things can't get worse." Emily said this to Jessica as she lifted her away from a rust-colored dumpster she'd decorated with vomit. "Your body's rejected the poison from the alcohol. Should be a cinch from here."

Jessica shook her head. "No." She tumbled into a brick wall. "I got to get home. I'm totally sorry."

Emily rocked on her feet like a child in need of a potty break. "But Kristoff, he's all into me tonight. Bumped into me twice at the pool tables."

"I'll find my way home." The alley tilted. Jessica remembered a funhouse she'd negotiated as a child at the Lake County Fair. Her brain turned somersaults and she collapsed. Emily jammed her hands under her armpits and lifted her to her feet. She held her up as they wobbled toward the street. She propped her against a NO PARKING sign and asked to use her phone. Jessica said, "Ran out of juice when I was on the toilet, playing the bubble game."

"I see." Emily rummaged through her purse.

Headlights paled the women and a yellow cab pulled to the curb. The passenger window buzzed down and the driver leaned over the seat. "Hey ladies," he said. "Need a ride?"

Jessica grabbed the NO PARKING sign and reached for the back door. Emily stopped her. "Dude's, like, way past old. Gray hair. Black clothes. Only serial killers dress like that." She ducked to speak with the cabbie. "We're waiting for an Uber."

The cabbie laughed. "I'm right here. Cheaper and safer." He pointed to a laminated card posted on the glovebox with his name and photo. Looked like a mug shot.

"We'll stick with progress, if you don't mind." Emily slapped the roof of the cab and told the driver to move along. He peered over his wire-framed grandpa glasses, reminded Jessica of her father any time she said something he deemed stupid. Finally, Emily said, "We need to get the cops?"

Shaking his head, the cabbie chuckled once more. He turned the taxi around and parked at O'Neal's, a pub across the street.

Emily found her phone and ordered an Uber. She grumbled about the price. The door to the bar opened and Kristoff Novak, a DJ she'd been trying to bag for a couple of weeks, poked his head out. "You girls okay? Brummer and I were thinking of heading to the gardens at Valpo to smoke a bowl and look at the sky. Listen to some tunes, yo."

"Sounds awesome." Emily positioned Jessica against the NO PARKING sign again. "You going to be cool?" She gave her a kiss on the cheek and started for the bar. "I don't want to miss this." Then she stepped inside and left Jessica in the cold.

The sidewalk rocked like a boat on Lake Shafer as Jessica's head rolled back and forth. A compact car, looked like a purple Prius, rolled up. The driver yelled from his side, "Hey there!"

Jessica tumbled into the street, caught herself on the bumper, and inched her way to the driver's window. "You the Uber guy?"

She hoped she hadn't slurred too much. She'd heard stories about grabby jerks molesting lit passengers. This one didn't look too awful, though—young, lumberjack beard, long hair tied in a bun on the top of his head.

He said, "Name's Brian." He unlocked the back door and nodded over his shoulder. "People I like? They call me Junior."

Jessica got in. The vehicle smelled like mildew on cardboard. She gave him her address. "Just outside Lublin," she said. "It's easy to find." As the car merged into traffic, she noticed a baseball bat on the passenger seat. Seemed like it'd been smeared with blood.

The driver took a deep breath. He turned on the radio. "Kind of music you into?"

"Whatever's good," she said.

Dubstep pounded the speakers. The driver shouted something Jessica couldn't understand. He made eye contact with her in the rearview and smiled. Frankly, young guys with lumberjack beards had never bothered her. If they mustered the courage to approach her, they always looked down, as though embarrassed by their libidos.

The car picked up speed as the driver took the I-65 ramp toward Chicago. Not the way she would have chosen, but, oh well. The doors rattled as the music intensified. The exit for Lublin passed. Jessica tapped the driver on his shoulder. "You should have gotten off there."

He turned around, bobbed his head with the dubstep, the grin on his face growing as the car raced away from Lake County, toward Gary and Chicago beyond. Jessica looked for the driver's identification card. The dumbass didn't have a GPS or anything. He hadn't even pasted one of those Uber stickers to his window.

The driver took an exit just across the Illinois border, the last one before the first toll booth. Streetlights disappeared. Beech trees blotted out the sky. Darkness filled the Prius. Jessica cursed the possibility of having to walk home from there. She'd post a scathing review of the driver on the Internet the moment she plugged in her phone.

(2019)

Acknowledgements

Thanks to the following publications for hosting earlier versions of these stories: *All Due Respect*, *Flash Fiction Offensive*, *Guilty Crime Story Magazine*, *Indiana Crime 2015*, *Starlite Pulp Review*, *Switchblade Magazine*, and *Tough Magazine*.

Thanks to Jeremy Stabile and ABC Group Documentation for continuing to believe in my work.

Thanks to Jim Thomsen for his careful editing of this manuscript.

And thanks, as always, to my wife, Yuan, whose infinite love and patience is paralleled only by her skills as a proofreader.

Alec Cizak is a writer and filmmaker from Indiana.